THE
SECRET JOURNEY

Books by Peg Kehret

Cages
Danger at the Fair
Deadly Stranger
Horror at the Haunted House
Night of Fear
Nightmare Mountain
Sisters, Long Ago
The Richest Kids in Town
Terror at the Zoo
FRIGHTMARES™: Cat Burglar on the Prowl
FRIGHTMARES™: Bone Breath and the Vandals
FRIGHTMARES™: Don't Go Near Mrs. Tallie
FRIGHTMARES™: Desert Danger
FRIGHTMARES™: The Ghost Followed Us Home
FRIGHTMARES™: Race to Disaster
FRIGHTMARES™: Screaming Eagles
FRIGHTMARES™: Backstage Fright
The Blizzard Disaster
The Flood Disaster
The Volcano Disaster
The Secret Journey
My Brother Made Me Do It

Available from MINSTREL Books

THE
SECRET JOURNEY

PEG KEHRET

A MINSTREL® HARDCOVER
PUBLISHED BY POCKET BOOKS
New York   London   Toronto   Sydney   Singapore

A MINSTREL HARDCOVER

 A Minstrel Book published by
POCKET BOOKS, a division of Simon & Schuster Inc.
1230 Avenue of the Americas, New York, NY 10020

Library of Congress Cataloging-in-Publication Data

Kehret, Peg.
    The secret journey / Peg Kehret.
      p. cm.
    "A minstrel book."
    Summary: In 1834 when a storm at sea destroys the slave ship on which she is a stowaway, twelve-year-old Emma musters all her resourcefulness to survive in the African jungle.
    ISBN: 0-671-03416-2
    [1. Survival—Fiction. 2. Resourcefulness—Fiction. 3. Jungles—Fiction. 4. Ocean travel—Fiction.] I.Title.

PZ7.K2518 Sec 1999
[Fic]—dc21   99-042222

First Minstrel Books hardcover printing December 1999

10   9   8   7   6   5   4   3

For my granddaughters,
Chelsea Elizabeth Kehret
and Brett Michelle Konen,
with love from Moonie

CHAPTER

1

====⟨∅/∅⟩====

England
June 1834

Emma Bolton stood in the dark with her cheek pressed against the wall outside Mama's bedroom. She peered through the slim crack between the door and the wall, but could see only the kerosene lamp on the table beside Mama's bed.

She strained, trying to hear the whispered words. Even though Papa had left the door cracked open, he and the doctor spoke in such low tones that Emma caught only snatches of what was being said.

"Fresh air . . ." said Dr. Crissy. ". . . complete rest."

". . . survive the journey?" said Papa.

"No hope otherwise," said Dr. Crissy.

Emma shuddered. No hope? No hope that

Mama would get well and leave her bed and dance in the sunshine with Emma, the way she used to do? No hope that Mama and Emma would sit in the meadow and make wreaths of clover for their hair?

Emma wished she did not have to eavesdrop this way. Why couldn't Papa allow her to enter the bedroom, and hold Mama's hand, and hear the doctor's advice? Papa treated her as if she were a foolish toddler, rather than an almost-twelve-year-old young lady.

She's my mother, Emma thought. I deserve to know what's wrong with her and what's going to happen to her. But Emma knew better than to enter uninvited, or to ask questions.

Papa firmly believed that children should speak only when spoken to. Until Mama took sick, she was the parent who had usually spoken to Emma.

Emma knew that Papa loved her, in his own way. He just didn't know how to talk to her, or listen to her. And he surely did not know how to make clover wreaths or dance in the meadow.

The voices grew louder, and Emma realized that Papa and Dr. Crissy were walking toward the bedroom door. She scuttled down the hallway and into her own bedroom, leaving her door ajar so she could listen as Papa and Dr. Crissy passed.

"Tomorrow I'll book passage to Bordeaux," Papa said.

Bordeaux! Emma thought. Bordeaux is in France, hundreds of miles from here.

"She'll need a nurse," Dr. Crissy said. "The voyage will be hard on her."

"I'll ask Mattie to accompany us," Papa said.

"What about your girl?"

"Emma? My wife's older sister will be willing to take her, I think. She's a widow whose son, Odolf, is about Emma's age."

"No!" The word escaped from Emma's lips. Her hand flew to her mouth, too late to smother the exclamation.

"Emma!" Papa's voice was stern. "Come out here at once. How dare you hide in the dark and listen to our talk without permission?"

Emma stepped into the hallway, her head down. "I'm sorry, Papa," she said. "I only wanted to know how Mama is. I didn't mean to— Oh, Papa, please don't make me stay with Aunt Martha and Odolf. Please, Papa!"

"Hush," her father said. "I'll make the arrangements that I deem best for you."

"But you don't know what it's like when I'm there," Emma said. "Odolf is a bully. He teases and taunts, and Aunt Martha believes him when he says our arguments are all my fault. Oh, Papa, it's dreadful there, and besides, I want to stay with Mama."

"That's enough, Emma."

Emma could see she had made her father angry, but she was incapable of stopping. "Odolf is the meanest, most terrible boy I've ever known," Emma said. Tears trickled down both cheeks. "Mama says so, too. Mama would never want me to stay there."

"I said, that's enough! What your mama wants and what I want and what *you* want are not important. All that matters is that I get your mother to a warmer climate as quickly as possible. She's to have complete bed rest—which would never happen if you were with us."

"I'll stay away from her," Emma promised. "I'll be as quiet as a church mouse. I'll help cook and scrub. I'll—"

"You'll go to your aunt Martha's house, and you'll cause no trouble there," Papa said. His dark eyes flashed at Emma. "Do you understand me, Emma? You will do as you are told with no further argument."

"Yes, sir."

The tight line of Papa's lips softened slightly. "I'm sorry it has to be this way, but we must do what is best for your mother."

"How long will I have to stay there?"

"I don't know," Papa said.

Dr. Crissy and Papa exchanged a glance that sent a chill down the back of Emma's neck. A long time, their eyes seemed to say. You will be there a long, long time.

"Go to bed now, Emma."

"Yes, Papa."

Emma put on her nightdress, climbed into bed,

and blew out the candle, but she did not sleep. How could she? She lay in the dark, listening to the tick-ticking of the hall clock, and planning ways to avoid going to Odolf's house.

Plan Number One: She could pretend to be sick. Perhaps if she stopped eating and stayed in bed, as Mama had, Papa would take her to France, too.

She wasn't at all sure she would be able to fool Dr. Crissy, nor was she sure she would be able to starve herself for long. Emma had a hearty appetite; if Mattie tempted her with a tray of fried potatoes and mutton, or better still, rice pudding, she knew she could never refuse.

Plan Number Two: She would become a housemaid. Emma imagined herself scrubbing floors, lugging hot water up stairs, and—worst of all—emptying chamber pots. She quickly abandoned Plan Number Two.

Plan Number Three: She would go to the Christian Orphans' Home, pretend to have no parents, and declare herself ready to lead a life of service and sacrifice.

The trouble with that plan was that Emma was not ready to rise at five each morning for prayer. Nor was she eager to eat thin gruel twice a day, or wear hand-me-downs, or beg God to forgive her for her sins. As far as Emma knew, she had not committed any sins, so why should she ask forgiveness?

The religious life, she decided, might be even worse than living with Odolf.

Plan Number Four came to her just as she was dozing off. Her eyes flew open and she sat upright, clutching the bedclothes to her chest.

"Oh, my," Emma whispered, for she recognized instantly that besides being dangerous, this plan involved committing those very sins she had so smugly declared herself free of moments earlier.

She would have to steal, and lie, and disobey her father, none of which she had ever done nor ever wanted to do before.

Yet Emma knew, with no hint of hesitation, that this was the plan she would follow if Papa sent her to live with Aunt Martha and Odolf.

God will forgive me, she told herself. But will Papa?

CHAPTER

2

⟞—⟝

THE NEXT DAY Papa sent and received several messages. Emma knew that he was "making the arrangements that he deemed best."

Her worst fears were confirmed after dinner when Papa called her into his study.

"Your mama and I and Mattie will sail at high tide on Tuesday," he said, "aboard the *Wayfarer*, bound for the south of France."

"When is high tide?" Emma asked.

Papa scowled at the interruption. "High tide is around ten in the morning. We will leave for the docks at seven. The ship's captain, Captain Forbes, is an acquaintance of mine. He'll see that your mother is comfortable."

Emma wanted to say, "What about me?" but she held her tongue and waited.

"You will leave Monday afternoon," Papa said. "Your uncle will bring a buggy for you and your belongings. Have your clothes clean and your trunk packed when he arrives."

A flame of hope flared in Emma's mind. Maybe she was being sent to stay with Mama's younger brother, Uncle Edward, who lived alone in London.

Mama had nearly burst with pride when Uncle Edward was selected as one of the first men in the new civilian police force, and when he came to visit a month or so later, Emma was dazzled by the handsome young man in his blue tailcoat and stout top hat. Life in Uncle Edward's household would be pleasant indeed, though not so pleasant as staying with Mama.

Her hopes were quickly extinguished as Papa continued, "Edward will be here at three o'clock sharp on Monday to see your mother. Then he will drive you to Liverpool, to your aunt Martha's house. See that you're ready when he arrives."

"How much clothing shall I take with me?" Emma asked.

"Take everything. Mattie's daughter has agreed to come Tuesday afternoon, to close up the household."

Everything. If she was to take everything, it was clear to Emma that Papa had no idea when—or if—she would return.

She could tell that Papa expected her to argue

or to ask more questions, but Emma only nodded her head and said nothing. It didn't matter what arrangements Papa had made, because Emma had a different plan.

She would never, ever go to live at Odolf's house unless she were dragged there with her hands and feet tied, and she did not intend to give anyone the opportunity to do that.

While she did not relish the idea of disobeying Papa, her place was with Mama, and that was where Emma intended to be. If Papa refused to book passage for Emma on the *Wayfarer*, then Emma would board the ship herself.

Her stomach flip-flopped when she tried to picture Papa's reaction after he discovered she had run away from Aunt Martha's house and hidden on the ship to Bordeaux. By then it would be too late for him to send her back to Aunt Martha and the repulsive Odolf. By then the ship would be asail.

With luck, Emma thought, she would not be discovered until the second or third day—much too far into the journey for the captain to consider turning back to Liverpool.

Alone in her room Emma studied a map. The *Wayfarer* would travel from Liverpool down through St. George's Channel to the Atlantic Ocean. It would continue south past Spain and Portugal, and through the Strait of Gibraltar to Bordeaux. She did not know how long it would take.

On Monday after breakfast Papa said, "You may come with me to your mama's bedroom to tell her goodbye, but you are not to weep or to say anything that will upset her."

Emma nodded and followed her father up the stairs and into Mama's dimly lit bedroom.

Mama's face was pale, and her thick dark hair lay limply on the pillow as if it were too tired to curl around her face. Mama's hollow cheeks and the dark smudges under her eyes startled Emma. She had known Mama was sick, but she had not expected Mama to look so different. Her arms were as slender as broomsticks; blue veins stood out on her translucent hands.

Fear clutched Emma's heart. What if the fresh air and sunshine didn't help? What if Mama didn't get well?

"Hello, Mama," Emma said. "It's me. Emma."

Mama's eyelids fluttered open, and the corners of her lips curved into a smile. "My darling girl," she murmured, the words sounding as soft as rose petals.

"I came to say goodbye, Mama."

"Be a good girl while I'm gone. Help your aunt Martha."

"I'll be good," Emma promised, though she knew she would not be helping Aunt Martha.

"Goodbye, sweet Emma," Mama said. "I'll miss you."

"I'll see you soon, Mama," Emma said, and then feared she had given away her secret.

10

Mama only closed her eyes and whispered, "I hope so."

"Come along, Emma," Papa said. "Your mother needs to rest now."

Emma followed her father from the room, more convinced than ever that she must go to France with her parents.

When her father reached the door to Emma's room, he stopped. "I will miss you, too, Emma," he said. "You are a good daughter."

Shocked speechless by that statement, Emma could only stare.

Papa bent and kissed her lightly on the cheek. "Finish your packing now," he said.

Emma nodded and went into her room. It seemed odd to fold her clothes and put them in the trunk when she knew she would not be taking them out again. She had decided that her chances of getting aboard the *Wayfarer* would be greater if she looked like a boy. Although Odolf was bigger than Emma, she intended to stow away wearing his clothes.

When Uncle Edward arrived that afternoon, Emma was ready.

"Be a good girl," Papa said. "Do as you're told and do not pester your aunt with questions." He paused a moment and then added, "And try to get along with your cousin."

Mattie burst into tears and flung her arms around Emma. "I'll miss my little dove," she sobbed as she held Emma close to her ample chest.

Not for long, Emma thought.

She disentangled herself from Mattie's damp embrace and climbed into the buggy. Uncle Edward entertained her with stories of life in London during the two-hour ride to Liverpool, and Emma was grateful for his chatter. She wished he would be spending the night at Aunt Martha's house.

Odolf awaited her arrival, a smirk on his round face. Emma was sure he had planned some torment for her on her first evening there.

"Be a gentleman and carry your cousin's trunk to her room," Uncle Edward said.

Grumbling, Odolf lifted the trunk. After saying goodbye to her uncle, Emma trailed after Odolf, curious to see which room Aunt Martha had chosen for her. Not that it mattered, since she would reside there only a few hours.

"You know why we're taking you in, don't you?" Odolf asked.

When Emma did not reply, he answered his own question. "It's because your father is paying us to look after you. If it weren't for the money, my mother would have said *no*."

"What a pity," Emma said, "that you are so needy." As soon as the unkind words left her mouth, she regretted them. Aunt Martha had married a coal porter, and when he died of cholera two years later, she and baby Odolf were left in dire financial straits. Emma knew that Mama and Papa often helped with Aunt Martha's expenses, but Mama had taught her not to mention that to Odolf. "Never flaunt your good fortune," Mama said. But Odolf made her so angry!

Odolf's face flushed red. "We are not needy," he declared.

He dropped her trunk on the floor, aiming for Emma's toe. She stepped aside before the trunk hit her.

"Starting tomorrow you'll attend school with me," Odolf said.

"At the national school?" Emma had never attended a public school.

Odolf nodded, pleased by her surprise. "I've already alerted the teacher that you are a known troublemaker."

Ordinarily such a remark would have made Emma furious. She was quick to learn and had never received a negative report about her lessons. Well, perhaps her governess had mentioned once or twice that Emma could be less impetuous and headstrong, but being impetuous and headstrong were not the same as being a troublemaker.

Today Odolf's comment didn't anger her because Emma knew what Odolf could not know: she would not be attending public school with him.

"How thoughtful of you to talk to the teacher," Emma replied. She smiled sweetly and added, "No doubt he believes such troublemaking traits run in our family."

Odolf glared at her for a moment, then said, "It must be difficult to know that your father and mother do not want you with them."

"They *do* want me," Emma said. She turned away, not wanting Odolf to see the tears that had sprung to her eyes at the truth of his words. "They must do what's best for Mama's health."

"My mother says you'll be with us for half a year at least, and much longer if your mother does not survive the consumption."

Consumption? Papa's sister had died of consumption last year. No wonder Papa was so distraught.

Shocked and furious that Odolf knew what was wrong with Mama when she did not, Emma cried, "She *will* survive!"

"Perhaps not. Mother says maybe you'll never return home."

Angered by his cold-hearted remarks, Emma said, "Then the teacher will have ample time to find out who is a troublemaker—and who is a liar."

Odolf lunged at Emma, grabbed her wrist, and twisted her arm behind her. "Take that back," he demanded. "Say I'm not a liar."

Emma gritted her teeth and refused to speak. Odolf bent her arm farther, sending jolts of pain from Emma's wrist to her shoulder.

"Take it back!"

He's going to break my arm, Emma thought, and then I won't be able to run away and find the *Wayfarer*. "You are not a liar," she mumbled.

He gave her arm another painful twist. "Say it louder."

"You are not a liar."

"That's better." Odolf dropped her wrist, looking pleased with himself.

Emma glared at him as she rubbed her throbbing arm. "Those who tell falsehoods," she said, "are always found out."

Odolf turned and stomped out of the room. Good riddance, Emma thought. She stayed in her room until she was called to dinner, watching out the narrow window to see in which direction the sun would set.

As they ate, Aunt Martha seemed almost too glad to have Emma there. She smiled at nothing and talked constantly, as if this were a happy visit of Emma's choosing. Emma tried to be polite, but the nervous chatter made her edgy.

Her heart felt heavy with the knowledge of Mama's illness. But not so heavy that she didn't enjoy the hearty oxtail soup, some pickled oysters, and a large portion of raspberry fool.

It was kind of Aunt Martha to prepare Emma's favorite dessert, and she felt a momentary pang of remorse at her intentions, until she saw Odolf lick raspberry juice off his grubby finger and then stick the same finger back into the serving bowl.

Emma asked to be excused from the table.

"Sleep well," Aunt Martha said. "I'll wake you in time to have breakfast before you and Odolf leave for school."

"Thank you for your kindness, Aunt Martha."

"I am pleased to have you here, more pleased than I can tell you."

With Aunt Martha still gushing, Emma headed for the sanctuary of her own small room.

Odolf scowled at her.

Alone in her room, Emma sat on the edge of her bed, imagining Odolf's surprise the next morning. She wondered if he would be happy to be rid of her or disappointed that he would not have her around to pester.

Fearful that she would not wake up in time to get away unnoticed, Emma did not go to bed Monday night.

At midnight when the rest of the household was silent, Emma crept into the kitchen. She took half a loaf of bread, a wedge of cheese, and the last two apples from the barrel.

Back in her room she removed clean undergarments from her trunk, then tied them and the food into a bundle. Last she tiptoed down the hall to Odolf's bedroom.

She slowly nudged the door open, relieved to hear his deep, even breathing. She wished she dared to light a candle, but she feared that even such a small light would disturb his sleep. Putting her hands against the wall, she moved slowly around the room until she found a group of three hooks with clothing dangling from each. Emma felt the clothing, trying to determine what each piece was.

Her fingers recognized a pair of trousers and then a linen shirt. The shirt had a distinctive odor; Emma lifted it to her nose and sniffed. Ugh! Clearly, Odolf had worn this garment more than once and the idea of putting it against her skin was distasteful in the extreme.

She groped more, hoping to come across an armoire that contained a supply of clean shirts. Instead she stumbled on a pair of Odolf's boots and nearly fell. When the boots toppled over, Odolf shifted position. His breathing became more shallow.

I've awakened him, Emma thought. If he opens his eyes and finds me here, he'll . . .

The thought was too horrible to pursue. Emma dropped to her hands and knees. Still clutching the trousers and the offensive shirt, she crept out of the room.

CHAPTER

3

———⟨ⴰⴰⴰ⟩———

BACK IN THE safety of her own room, Emma tried on Odolf's clothes, relieved that they were only slightly too large for her.

I'll wear my chemise under the shirt, she decided. It will fill out the shirt, keep me warm, and prevent the smell of Odolf's sweat from soaking into my skin.

By candlelight, using her best penmanship, she wrote a note.

Dear Aunt Martha:

I hope my disappearance does not overly alarm you. While I thank you for offering to keep me with you, I cannot accept your hospitality. Since Odolf informed the teacher that I am a troublemaker, I fear for my reception at school.

Emma paused, smiling briefly as she imagined Aunt Martha questioning Odolf about his fib. Odolf will deny it, Emma thought, and Aunt Martha will believe him. Her smile faded.

Therefore, I have gone to stay with a trusted friend where I will be safe and looked after until Papa and Mama return. Please do not waste your time searching for me.

Your loving niece,
Emma

Emma blotted the ink carefully and laid the note on her bed where her aunt would find it when she came to wake Emma the next morning.

By then, Emma thought, I'll be at the docks. I'll have asked questions and figured out a way to board the ship without being noticed. By then I will be snugly hidden somewhere on the *Wayfarer*, waiting for the anchor to be raised.

When the hall clock chimed three, Emma tucked her hair into the cap Odolf had left on the hat rack, then tiptoed down the stairs and out the door. She closed it quietly and set off in the direction of the sunset.

She had never been to the docks, but she knew

her geography. The bay had to be on the west side of Liverpool. If she headed west, she would surely find her way.

Emma was amazed at how much easier it was to walk in trousers. Her legs felt weightless as she strode down the cobblestone streets. Think how well she would be able to dance! Why do women continue to wear bulky hoop skirts and endless petticoats, she wondered, when trousers were far more comfortable?

She imagined Mama in trousers, twirling and laughing. She also tried to imagine Papa's reaction but was unable to do so.

Smiling at the image of herself and Mama wearing trousers as they danced in the meadow, Emma left Aunt Martha's well-kept neighborhood.

Instead of tidy homes with gardens out in front, she now passed ramshackle tenements with garbage piled where grass should be. The gas lamps that illuminated the streets near Aunt Martha's house did not continue. A half-moon cast eerie shadows as she hurried westward.

A scrawny dog barked and snarled from the steps of one building. Emma usually liked dogs, but this one caused her to cross to the other side of the street. She kept a wary eye on the animal until she was well past it.

A row of narrow houses huddled together, their dark doorways gaping like black caves. As Emma hurried past them, a rat scuttled out of one of the doorways and ran right in front of her.

"Oh!" Emma gasped as she watched the creature's skinny tail disappear behind an overturned cart.

Raucous laughter came from an alehouse on the corner ahead. The sharp, pungent smell of rum drifted on the wind. Emma slowed her pace and considered whether to continue straight west.

As she hesitated, angry shouts suddenly filled the night. Brawling bodies spilled into the street, surrounding her. Scrambling to get out of the way, Emma collided with a burly man who grabbed her shirt collar, spat in the street, and demanded to know why she didn't watch where she was going.

"I'm sorry, sir," Emma said. "I did not intend to bump into you."

He let go of her collar and leaned closer to her. "Hey, men!" he called. "Look what I have here. It's a fine-sounding lad, it is, and not one of us, that's sure."

"If you'll excuse me, sir," Emma said, "I'll be going now." She walked away as she spoke, but a second man quickly blocked her path. "You ain't excused," he said.

Sensing her nervousness, the group quit fighting among themselves and formed a horseshoe around Emma, forcing her to back up until she was standing against the front of the alehouse.

21

The lot of them looked as if their clothing had come from a rag fair, and many a Saturday night had passed since they had been close to warm water and soap. Her stomach turned like a child's hoop as their collective stench surrounded her.

"What's in your bundle?" the first man asked.

"Only some clean clothing," Emma replied.

"Let's have a look." He reached for the bundle, but Emma held it behind her. It was all the food she had, and it might have to last her for several days. Also if the men saw her undergarments, they would know she was a girl, not a boy.

"None would fit you, sir," she said. "You are large and strong, while I am small and skinny."

One man leaned close to Emma's face. "Small and pretty," he said. "A pretty boy."

Emma stared at the unshaven thug. His breath, hot on her cheek, reeked of rum; she tried not to inhale.

"*Too* pretty," said another man, who had a dirty handkerchief tied around his neck. He reached out and snatched the cap from Emma's head. Her hair cascaded to her shoulders.

"Well, lookee here," said the man with the handkerchief. "Our pretty boy isn't a boy at all." He removed a shapeless felt hat from his head and bowed low in front of Emma, sweeping the hat across his boots.

Emma struggled to keep her legs from shaking. "I'll thank you to return my cap," she said as she held out her hand.

"How old are you, lass?" asked the first man, the one she had bumped into.

"Age makes no difference," said the man who had Emma's cap. "If she's old enough to be out by herself in the dark of night, she's old enough to go inside with us and drink to the glory of England." He plopped the cap on his own head and crooked his arm toward Emma, as if she should hold it while they walked inside together.

Emma's thoughts raced. What can I do? she wondered. I must escape from these ruffians, or there's no telling what will happen to me.

"Hear, hear!" shouted the man with the handkerchief. "Let's all drink to the glory of England."

Emma raised her hand and pointed over the shoulders of the men. "Look!" she cried. "Here comes my uncle, Lord Whitehead, cousin of the king." She waved her hand wildly, wondering how such a nonexistent name had popped into her imagination. "Your Highness! Here I am, Uncle!"

The men turned to look where Emma was waving. Instantly she grabbed her cap from the head of the man who wore it, ducked around the end of the building, and ran.

"Where's the king's cousin? I don't see any lord."

"And I don't see any girl. She's gone!"

"You let her get away, you oaf."

"Who's an oaf? Watch your blathering mouth."

The shouts quickly escalated into another brawl, and Emma knew that instead of following her, the drunken men were fighting among themselves again.

As she ran, Emma jammed the cap on her head and stuffed her hair under it. Her eyes darted back and forth across the street in front of her, watching for any sign of further trouble.

She ran until a kink in her side forced her to stop and catch her breath. She stood doubled over, holding her side, and waited for her pounding heart to return to its normal rhythm.

"Ssst."

Emma straightened and whirled around to see where the sound had come from.

"Ssst. Over here."

CHAPTER

4

—❦❦❦—

SHE SAW THE dark outline of a small figure, sitting cross-legged in the dirt. Looking closer, she saw that it was a boy, only six or seven years old.

"Do you have any jobs I can do for money?" the boy asked.

"Where do you live?"

"Here. There. Nowhere in particular."

"You mean, you have no home?"

"The streets are my home. All of Liverpool. 'Tis better than living indoors with a father who beats me."

Emma shuddered. Despite Papa's strictness and his disinterest in Emma's affairs, he had never struck her.

"I'm hungry," the boy said.

"I have no money," Emma said. "But I could give you a small chunk of bread and a bit of cheese."

"I don't take handouts." The boy got to his feet. "I'll work for you, miss, and gladly. Just tell me what you need."

Emma thought a moment. "I need one thing," she said. "I'm looking for a sailing ship called the *Wayfarer*. It sails at high tide this morning. Could you lead me to it—or at least to the docks?"

The boy smiled so broadly that his teeth gleamed in the dim moonlight. "I don't know the names of the vessels," he said, "but I can take you to the docks. Follow me."

The boy walked quickly. Even in trousers Emma had to hurry to keep up with him. She was shocked by the squalid living quarters they passed. Uncle Edward had spoken of slums and shantytowns in London and Liverpool, but she had not imagined anything this miserable.

The boy suddenly slowed and pointed. "That's where I used to live," he said. "In that cellar."

The stench of unburied garbage was sickening. Maybe the boy *is* better off on his own, Emma thought. She promised herself that once Mama was well again, she would speak to Papa about doing something to improve the living conditions of these unfortunate souls.

Soon they passed different types of buildings—

warehouses and factories—and then the boy said, "Smell the sea air?"

Emma drew a deep breath, knowing she was near her destination.

The first faint light of dawn hovered over the bay as the boy said, "Here you be."

Water stretched endlessly before her. Emma had known the ocean was large, but this seemed to go on forever. She wondered why Papa and Mama had never brought her to see it. True, it was a long way from home, but they could have come on one of their visits to Aunt Martha.

Dozens of ships lined the docks along the bay, and she was struck by a new fear: what if she did not find the *Wayfarer* in time?

She untied her pack, removed the bread, and gave the boy a hunk the size of her fist.

He chewed greedily while she tried to break off a piece of the cheese.

"You need a knife," he said, and promptly produced one from a sheath inside one of his stockings. He cut a corner from the cheese, taking more than Emma had intended to give him, but she did not protest. She would have ship's food to eat in a few days; she could only guess when or what this child would eat next.

"I'll share one of my apples with you," she said. She had planned to save the apples, but watching the boy eat aroused not only her pity, but her own appetite.

He quickly cut the apple in two and took one half.

"I need to find my ship now," Emma said as she retied her bundle. "Thank you for showing me the way."

"Is the *Wayfarer* one of the Black Ball ships?" the boy asked.

"I don't know. What are they?"

"The Black Ball line sails packet ships to America and back. Liverpool merchants send cutlery and fine cotton and woolen goods to America each month. In return they get raw cotton for their looms. They also carry passengers. The packet ships are the fastest ships on the sea."

"How do you know so much about sailing ships?"

"I spend most mornings on the docks. Passengers are often willing to pay for an errand boy." He finished his half of the apple. "If I were going to hide on a ship, I'd go on a Black Baller."

"Who said anything about hiding?" Emma said.

"Passengers with tickets know where to go."

"I'm not sailing to America," Emma said. "I'm going to the south of France."

"Do you have a weapon?" the boy asked.

Surprised by the question, she shook her head, no.

"Here." He handed her his knife.

"I can't take that. You need it."

"I can get another. You might need to defend yourself."

Emma hesitated for an instant, remembering the drunken thugs who had surrounded her. She tried to imagine herself using the knife in self-defense, and knew she could not do it.

"No," she said. "Thank you for the offer, but you keep it."

The boy returned the knife to his stocking.

"Good-bye," Emma said. "Thank you for helping me."

"Beware the packet rats," he said. "They'd as soon rob a passenger as not."

Having no idea what a packet rat was, Emma did not respond. She walked away from him toward the docks. Sea birds swooped noisily overhead as waves crashed rhythmically against the moored ships.

Even this early in the morning, the docks were busy. Men loaded cargo. Small fishing boats prepared to leave for the day.

Emma saw two men hoisting barrels on to a wooden cart. She approached them and said, "Excuse me. Can you tell me which ship is the *Wayfarer*?"

The men stopped their work and eyed her. "Who wants to know?" the taller man asked.

"I do. My parents sail on the *Wayfarer* at high tide today."

"If they're sailing on it, boy, they can tell you where to find it."

"They—they do not know I am here," Emma said.

"If you're thinking of stowing away," the man said, "put the idea out of your head."

"I'm not trying to stow away," Emma said, feeling the color rise in her cheeks as she spoke. Why did everyone she met immediately guess her plan? Were her intentions that obvious? "I only want to see them off."

The man nodded. "See that small vessel?" he said. "The third one over, flying the black flag with the lightning bolt on it?"

"Yes."

"That's the ship you want."

"Thank you, sir," Emma said and then added, "Can you tell me what a packet rat is?"

Both men howled with laughter. "Him!" they said in unison, each pointing to the other, then laughed again.

"Our vessel's called a packet ship," the shorter man explained.

Emma mumbled, "I see," and left. The boy had said something about packet ships; she should have figured out that a packet rat was a crewman on such a ship, instead of embarrassing herself by asking the question of those very crewmen. Mama's advice echoed in her mind: Think before you speak, Emma. Don't blurt out whatever comes into your head.

I must be more careful, Emma thought. Mistakes such as that only call attention to myself and make me more memorable if Aunt Martha should come asking for me.

She knew that as soon as her note was discovered, Aunt Martha would begin searching for her, and she worried that Aunt Martha or Odolf would think to look for her at the docks.

As she hurried away from the two men, the short man poked the tall one. "What's the matter with you, steering the boy wrong that way?" he asked.

"A lad his age has no business stowing away."

"He's clearly an innocent, with no knowledge of the sea or its people."

"All the more reason not to sneak on board."

"Maybe he really is here to see his parents off."

"If that were true, his parents would be with him."

Shaking his head, the second man watched Emma hurry toward the ship she'd been shown. "I pity the poor lad if he sets sail aboard the *Black Lightning*," he said. "Why did you direct him toward the most evil ship in the harbor?"

"It's a punishment for telling lies," the first man said.

The second man hoisted a barrel on to the cart. "Seems harsh justice to me," he said. *"The Black Lightning* isn't fit for a mule to sail on, much less a boy of tender age."

"I survived my first voyage at that age, and so did you."

"Not on the *Black Lightning.* Not with Isaac Bacon as captain."

"The lad will be a man by the time he reaches Africa."

"If he lives that long."

CHAPTER

5

———⟨⟨⟨⟩⟩⟩———

Emma made her way around stacks of cargo waiting to be loaded. The first ship she passed had a big black circle on the largest sail and another on its top flag. She realized it was one of the Black Ball line.

She eyed with interest the long, narrow ship with its V-shaped bottom and sharp bow. Its shape must be what made it so speedy. She wished Papa had chosen this handsome vessel.

Emma hurried on, growing more nervous by the minute. What if Aunt Martha came searching for her and spotted her before she could get on board? Judging from the amount of daylight, it was past seven. Papa and Mama and Mattie were on their way; Emma had to be on board before they got here.

Her worries rolled in her head like the wheels of Papa's buggy. What if she couldn't manage to sneak on board? If she did get on board, what if she got caught before the ship left the harbor?

Emma tried to push her fears out of her mind. Worrying about what might happen did no good. Instead she tried to think of the happy future, when Mama would be well enough to be out of bed. Emma hoped the next few weeks would pass quickly. Once they were all together in France, she was sure Papa would forgive her, but in the meantime, she knew she must face not only possible punishment by the ship's captain, but the full force of Papa's anger when he found that she had disobeyed him and come along on the voyage.

As she approached the ship on which she was to sail, she became more and more uneasy. She wondered if Papa had actually seen this vessel before he booked passage. Most of the ships in the harbor had billowing white sails, shiny hulls, and flags flying high. This one's paint was so badly peeled that the original color was unrecognizable and the lettering of its name was no longer legible. The dingy gray sails and weathered wood made the vessel seem unclean and somehow less sturdy than the others.

With growing dismay she reached the part of the dock nearest the ship and stood looking out at it.

It was not like Papa, Emma thought, to accept

anything but the best, especially where Mama's health was concerned. Perhaps it was the only ship headed for France. It was important to get Mama there as quickly as possibly; maybe there had been no choice on such short notice.

It won't be for long, she told herself. I can endure a cramped cabin, if I have to, and if our quarters are unclean, Mattie will scrub them. Even this ship would still be better than months and months with Odolf.

A crew of men hustled up and down the plank, loading the cargo. Emma's consternation grew as she watched the crew. All were tough, vicious-looking seamen, worse even than the street brawlers she had encountered earlier. Most of the sailors seemed drunk; their language as they shouted to one another made Emma blush. One man toppled to the ground and, apparently unconscious, was carried on board and dumped on deck.

Again Emma wondered if Papa had actually come here and inspected this vessel. Maybe it's better on the inside, she thought. And maybe this crew is only loading the cargo, not sailing with us. She could not imagine any friend of Papa's hiring such ruffians.

As the sun rose higher, the docks filled with people. An old woman with a charcoal stove sold hot apples. A milkmaid passed, carrying a shoulder yoke with cans of milk hanging from each side. Vendors sold baskets, rat traps, and fish.

Horse-pulled carts rumbled by, and passengers for the ship next to hers began to arrive, along with their luggage.

Two young boys, chased by a dog, played tag. No one noticed Emma as she waited for a chance to slip on board without being seen.

With sticks and much shouting, the rough crewmen drove three squealing pigs up the plank. Emma realized that the pigs would provide fresh meat during the voyage.

After penning the pigs, all but one of the crew stayed on board. That one returned to the dock and picked up a wooden crate containing chickens.

The chickens squawked, white feathers fluttering to the ground. One chicken stuck its beak between two slats of the crate and pecked the sailor's fingers. Swearing, the man dropped the crate and stuck his bleeding finger in his mouth.

When the crate hit the stone street, the wood splintered, the crate broke open, and eight frightened chickens ran off, flapping their wings. The boys' dog gave chase.

The sailor dived for the closest chicken and captured it, but there was no way he could hang on to it and catch the other chickens at the same time. The crate, in pieces, was clearly unusable.

"Hey, there! You boys!" he called to the youngsters who had stopped playing tag to watch the spectacle. "Help me get these chickens on board, and there'll be a farthing for you."

Each boy ran after a chicken—and Emma saw her chance. She dashed toward one of the chickens, scooped it up, and held it at arm's length from her body with its head facing away from her so it couldn't peck her. Both of the boys had also caught a chicken, and when they followed the sailor up the plank to the ship, Emma went, too.

The chickens were turned loose on the ship's deck. The boys held out their hands. "We'll take our farthing now," one said.

"Begone with you," the sailor said. "I've no coins to spare."

"You promised!" one of the boys said. "You said if we caught your chickens, you'd give us a farthing."

"And four of my chickens are still cackling and clucking on the dock," the sailor replied. "There's no pay for half a job."

"We'll catch the others," one boy said and the boys ran down the plank, the sailor close behind.

Emma quietly backed away until she reached a stairway that led below. She climbed down, walked through a dark, narrow passageway, and saw the perfect hiding place.

A stack of straw leaned against the wall on one side of the passageway, with a pile of blankets beside it. Emma carefully pushed the bottom of the straw away from the wall, creating enough space for her to fit in. The stiff straw scratched her face and hands; she was glad she had on Odolf's long-sleeved shirt to protect her arms.

When she had created a small tunnel between the straw and the wall, she draped a blanket over her shoulders and backed into the space.

As soon as she was completely behind the straw, she pulled the blanket over her head, hoping that the dark blanket against the dark wall in the dark passageway would not be noticed.

She assumed the straw would be used as bedding material for the pigs and any other animals that had been brought along. Perhaps there was a cow on board, too, to provide milk for the passengers. The straw would likely be removed from the pile a little each day, so Emma felt her hiding place was secure for as long as she needed it.

Her legs soon ached from her cramped position, but Emma did not dare to move. Twice sailors hurried past. Each time she held her breath, fearful that they might notice her, but they were intent on their work.

By now Aunt Martha would have found her note. Emma regretted the worry she was causing her aunt. She wondered if Mama and Papa had been notified of her absence before they left home. She hoped not. Her greatest fear was that Papa would suspect her plan, search the ship, and find her before they set sail.

No matter when she was discovered, she knew Papa would be furious, and she was sorry for that. But Emma felt he should not have put her in a position where she had to run away. Why didn't Papa *care* that Odolf would make Emma's life miserable? And why didn't he see that Emma couldn't bear to be shut out of Mama's life, even if her life was one of sickness?

Did Papa think by shielding Emma from unpleasantness he made her life easier? If so, Papa was mistaken.

I would rather sit by Mama's death bed, Emma thought, than sit alone wondering and worrying, not knowing how she is. Not knowing was the worst feeling of all.

She heard the sailors call to one another, but she heard no passengers boarding. Their voices must be covered by the loud noises of the crew.

She had been in her hiding place only half an hour when one harsh voice rose above the rest. "Come alive, men!" he shouted. "Heave anchor!"

So soon? Emma thought. She didn't think it was ten o'clock yet—more like half-past eight. Surely the ship would not sail early, would it? What if Papa and Mama had not yet boarded? What if they delayed their departure so Papa could look for her, and arrived too late?

A new thought occurred to her: what if her disappearance had caused Mama and Papa to cancel their journey to France so that Papa could search for her? What if she were on board the *Wayfarer*, but Mama and Papa and Mattie were not?

On the deck above her a drunken voice burst into song. "Then blow ye winds southerly, southerly blow."

Other voices joined in the song: "We'll cross the equator, and onward we go."

Drunken fools, Emma thought. Why are they singing of the equator when the ship is bound for France? The equator was hundreds of miles farther, clear in the middle of Africa.

A different voice called, "Anchor's aweigh!"

Beneath her the ship creaked and groaned.

The floor shifted as the ship moved.

I must be wrong about the time, Emma thought. Papa had said he knew Captain Forbes personally; the captain would make certain that all passengers he knew were on board.

Cheers mingled with the singers' voices as they repeated their song, "Blow ye winds southerly, southerly blow."

We're off, Emma thought. For better or worse, I'm on board the *Wayfarer* with Mama and Papa, bound for France.

CHAPTER

6

⟞⟨∅∅⟩⟝

Emma's stomach churned. She guessed the ship had been under way for about three hours, although it was hard to keep track of time. From the way the vessel rose and fell, she knew they must have left behind the quiet waters of the bay and entered the Atlantic Ocean.

Each time the floor beneath her lifted, bile from her stomach rose into Emma's mouth. When the floor dropped, Emma fought the urge to vomit. Although she had felt hungry when she first settled into her spot behind the straw stack, she had decided to wait awhile before eating. Now she was glad that her stomach was empty.

Her problem was not helped by the stuffiness of her hiding place. With the wall on one side, the straw on the other, and the blanket pulled over her head, Emma breathed only stale air. The blanket smelled soiled, which made her stomach even more uneasy.

Perhaps worst of all, Emma badly needed to relieve herself. She had no idea what sort of privy a ship had or where it would be, nor did she dare look for one. If she were discovered too soon, she worried that the captain might turn around and return her to Liverpool. Quarreling sailors passed her frequently.

She stayed crouched behind the straw with her eyes closed, hoping she would not vomit, and tried not to think about her discomfort.

Instead she planned what she would say to Papa after she was discovered, for she knew that she would eventually either be found or come out voluntarily. She decided her best tactic would be honesty. She began preparing a speech that she hoped would soften Papa's anger.

"I am sorry if I have distressed you, Papa, but I love you and Mama too much to be separated from you for such a long time. I could not bear to think of—"

Footsteps clomped toward her, stopping beside her pile of straw. Angry voices complained loudly.

"Straw, the captain says. Use straw for a mattress."

"Loose straw, at that. Not even tied."

"And look! There's not enough of it for half the crew."

"Then it's good we got here first."

Emma felt the straw above her slide forward and down as the men filled their arms and carried the straw off.

The voices continued, cursing the captain. More footsteps rushed to the scene.

"Give me some of that! You took too much!"

"Get your own."

They're going to take the whole straw stack right now, Emma thought. They're going to uncover me on the first day at sea.

She lay still, hoping that in the semidarkness no one would realize she was under the blanket.

She heard a scuffling sound and then a *thunk* as two men dropped to the floor, wrestling with each other. A boot kicked toward Emma, missing her face by only an inch. Trembling with fear and nausea, she huddled under the blanket and listened.

"On your feet!"

The men on the floor quit punching each other and stood up.

"There will be no fighting on the *Black Lightning*. Is that understood?"

"Yes, sir, Captain Bacon."

Black Lightning! Emma thought. *Captain Bacon!* She was certain Papa had said Captain Forbes.

"There will be no dinner for either of you

tonight," the voice continued. "Anyone else caught fighting has a one-way passage; you'll go to Cape Town with us, but you'll not see Liverpool again. Now put your straw and your blankets away and return to your posts. All of you."

There was silence except for one pair of feet walking away.

Then the grumbling began anew.

"It's going to be a hard trip, with that one in charge."

"He acts as if we were the slaves he's going after, instead of his crew."

Slaves? Emma thought. Slavery was abolished last year in the British Empire. How could the captain be going after slaves?

The ominous words repeated themselves in Emma's head: *Black Lightning.* Cape Town. Slaves. Captain Bacon. They blurred together as the horrible possibility awakened in her mind.

Could she be on the wrong ship? Instead of the *Wayfarer*, was she on a ship called *Black Lightning*—bound for Africa on an illegal journey?

The man at the dock had clearly pointed to this vessel, but she knew nothing of that man. Would he have lied to her? Why? For a joke? Just to be mean?

The idea that she might be on the wrong ship, terrible as it was, made sense. It explained the shoddy vessel and the ruffian crew that Emma had been sure Papa would not have selected. It explained why they set sail before ten o'clock, and why the sailors sang of going past the equator.

Her head throbbed as the reality of her situation sank in. Perhaps the reason she had not heard any passengers board was because there were no passengers. No Papa and Mama. No Mattie. No one to take her into a cabin for the remainder of the journey.

Just as Emma realized all the implications of her mistake, one of the men pulled away the blanket that covered her.

"Hey!" he said. "There's a boy here."

The men crowded around, staring down at her.

"Captain Bacon!" one of them shouted. "There's a stowaway on board!"

Emma's knees quivered as she stood up. She leaned against the wall, her head spinning with seasickness.

Perhaps it's good I've been discovered, she thought. If I'm on the wrong vessel, I'd rather go back to Liverpool even if it's too late to sail on the *Wayfarer*. Horrid as Odolf was, life with him would be better than going to Africa on a slave ship.

Fingers pointed at her as a tall man in a black coat, gold-colored vest, and wide-brimmed black hat strode toward her. Unlike the other men, he was clean shaven. When he spoke, she recognized the voice of Captain Bacon.

"What's your name, lad?" he asked.

"William," Emma replied.

"How old are you?"

"Twelve." That was almost the truth; her birthday was only three weeks off.

"Why are you here?"

"I was told this ship was the *Wayfarer.*"

The crewmen hooted with laughter.

"You were misinformed," said Captain Bacon. "This is the *Black Lightning*, bound for Cape Town, South Africa."

Images of jungles, wild animals, and huge poisonous snakes flashed through Emma's mind. "My parents are sailing on the *Wayfarer*," she said, "and I planned to accompany them."

"Without their knowledge or consent?" Captain Bacon said.

"My mother's gravely ill. I believe I can be of some help."

"You can help me," Captain Bacon said. "I need a ship's boy."

Emma blinked in disbelief. "But . . . but . . . aren't you going to take me back to Liverpool?"

The sailors guffawed.

"Why would I waste time sailing in the wrong direction?" Captain Bacon asked, though his words were not really a question.

"Because this ship is bound for Africa! I want to go to France."

"What you want is of no interest to me," Captain Bacon said. "You boarded this vessel voluntarily. Now you will earn your keep."

"What does the ship's boy do?"

The listening sailors nudged one another and laughed again.

"Whatever he's told," Captain Bacon said.

"How long will it take to reach Cape Town?" Emma asked.

"It depends on the weather. Three months, if we're lucky."

Emma struggled to keep tears from forming. Three months! And another three months to return to Liverpool. She was stuck with this heartless man and his ruffian crew for half a year.

One of the crew muttered, "We'll need plenty of luck. We're going at the worst time of year."

Captain Bacon ignored the comment and continued to address Emma. "Have you ever sailed?"

"No, sir."

"I command this ship," he said. "My orders are obeyed. Do you understand?"

"Yes, sir."

"I have the authority to bury the dead, to perform a marriage ceremony, and to kill in the event of a mutiny." He emphasized the last phrase, looking at the men rather than at Emma.

"I do not expect to need marriage or burial services," Emma said.

The crew snickered. A smile teased the corners of the captain's mouth.

Emma continued, "Nor will I participate in a mutiny."

"Are you armed, William?"

"No."

"You have no slingshot? A bowie knife? A weapon of any kind?"

"No, sir."

"Come with me. Today you'll learn to mend rigging. When that's done, you can go to the galley and peel potatoes. And wash dishes."

Emma followed the captain up the stairs to the deck, hoping the fresh air would calm her queasy stomach. The curious stares of the rough seamen set her nerves on edge.

I'm going to Africa, Emma thought. Africa! Oh, what have I done?

CHAPTER

7

———⟨ৡৡৡ⟩———

By TAKING DEEP breaths of fresh air, Emma got through the day without fainting or vomiting. Mr. Yule, the second mate, barked instructions for mending rigging. While the work was hard, Emma felt better on deck than she had when she was crouched behind the straw pile. It helped to find the privy, too.

In late afternoon Captain Bacon told her to report to Cook for the rest of the day. Cook was older than the rest of the crew and less harsh. Emma chopped onions, peeled and cut potatoes, and stirred the soup. The smell of food was almost more than she could bear.

"A bit seasick?" Cook asked.

Emma nodded. "Could I please have a cup of

hot tea with sugar and milk?" she asked. "It might settle my stomach."

Cook looked at her for a moment, then thrust a mug of thick black coffee into her hand. The bitter taste made Emma's lips pucker; she dumped the coffee into the slop pail.

When the meal had been served, Cook left. Emma washed the dishes by herself. Her whole body ached from her day's work. Blisters puffed between her thumbs and forefingers, the result of handling the rough rigging.

When the last dish was finally dried, Emma sneaked a sharp knife away from the galley, found an isolated section of deck, and chopped off her hair. She hacked it as close to her head as she dared without cutting her ears or neck. The long silky strands slid across her shoulders to the deck; Emma scooped them up and flung them overboard.

If she was to be the ship's boy, she needed to look like a boy. She could not depend on a cap to conceal her true identity, not with the wind blustering as it had all day.

A silver path of moonlight lay across the black water. Emma watched her hair float across the path and disappear into the darkness.

Good-bye, Emma, she thought. Hello, William.

She was too tired to care how she looked. She'd had no sleep at Odolf's house the night before, and now her eyelids drooped with weariness. She longed to crawl into her soft bed at home, pull the quilt snugly under her chin, and have Mama—a healthy, happy Mama—whisper from the doorway, "Good night, Emma. Sweet dreams, my darling girl."

Emma had asked Mr. Yule where she should sleep.

"Find yourself a bit of space," he replied, "where you won't get stepped on."

Where might that be? Emma wondered. In a pen with the pigs and the chickens?

She had also asked if it would really be three whole months before they saw land again.

"Could be longer," Mr. Yule said. "Many ships spend three months trying to reach Cape Town, and then give up."

"Give up! You mean, they turn back without reaching their destination?"

"The sea can defeat even determined sailors," he said. "We'll head into huge rolling waves, a thousand feet from crest to crest. We'll likely have heavy gales and sudden violent storms."

She hoped Mr. Yule was exaggerating, but he spoke so matter-of-factly that she feared his words were true.

When she returned the knife to the galley, she found an empty burlap sack. Draping it over her shoulders for a blanket, she curled up beside the potato bin with her head on her hands.

Tears leaked on to her fingers; she wiped her

cheeks with a corner of the rough burlap. How will I endure months of this? she wondered.

Too tired to cry for long, Emma fell asleep in the middle of her prayer for Mama's recovery.

Cook woke her at five o'clock to carry coffee to the men keeping watch. Her back ached from sleeping on the hard floor, and her muscles felt stiff and sore from yesterday's work. But sleep had refreshed her spirits, and she met the morning determined to make it to Cape Town, and then back to Liverpool.

Her stomach growled from hunger; the seasickness was gone. Emma helped Cook prepare and serve breakfast, but when her turn finally came to eat, the oatmeal was cold and the biscuits were gone. She sipped a small amount of coffee. The taste was terrible, but it quenched her thirst.

The ship's boy, Emma learned, was expected to do any jobs that nobody else wanted to do. She fed the livestock; she ladled beans onto plates; she scrubbed the decks.

There were no women on board, and since no one suspected that the ship's boy was really a ship's girl, Emma guarded her secret carefully. She missed Mama desperately, and said a prayer each morning and night for Mama's return to good health.

In between prayers Emma worked hard, obeyed orders, and talked as little as possible. When she was quiet, the sailors did not notice her. When she spoke, usually to ask a question, someone always gave her another job.

Fighting broke out frequently among the crew, but Emma learned to ignore the oaths and shouts. At night she listened to the men sing songs of the sea; soon she could sing along.

She dreaded preparing meals in the galley, when Cook gave her any task near the hot cooking fire. Emma preferred working on deck, where pleasant trade winds cooled her skin, but she quickly learned that any complaint only doubled her chores.

By keeping her mouth shut and her ears open, she learned the proper names for the ship parts. She learned which sailors to stay clear of, especially after dark, when the rum flowed.

An older sailor named Maury was kinder than the others. When he found Emma staring at the stars late one night, he leaned on the rail beside her and taught her the names of the constellations.

Maury told her the legend of Sagittarius, the archer. He pointed out Vega, which he said was one of the brightest stars in the whole sky. Emma's favorite constellation was Scorpius; because it had many bright stars, it was easy to find.

The stars seemed bigger here, and more dense than they were at home. Three weeks into the journey, on the night of Emma's twelfth birthday, Maury showed her the Southern Cross low in the sky. The sight was the only gift she received.

Emma remembered her joyous birthday celebration last year before Mama took sick. Pangs of homesickness and worry erased her excitement at seeing the Southern Cross for the first time. Feeling completely alone in the world, Emma looked away from the thousands of lights in the sky and went below to her sleeping place.

By then Emma had muscles instead of blisters, and she no longer cried herself to sleep. Each night she used a knife to make a small notch on the side of the potato bin. With no calendar, it was the only way she could keep track of the days.

The bin bore thirty-seven notches when the shout "Land Ho!" sent Emma scrambling up the stairs.

Mr. Yule gazed through his telescope. "Land directly east," he called.

Captain Bacon took the telescope and looked.

The ship rose and fell on huge waves.

Emma cupped her hands on the sides of her eyes and squinted in the direction Mr. Yule was facing. She saw only ocean.

"Where are we?" Emma asked Maury. "Are we at Cape Town already?"

"We're but halfway," he said, "rounding the bend along the coast of Liberia. We'll cross the equator soon. This is the closest to land we'll be until we reach the Cape of Good Hope."

"Why don't we stop?" Emma asked. "We could get fresh fruit and other supplies." And perhaps, she thought, I could board a different ship, going north.

Maury shook his head. "No port there," he said. "Nothing but jungle, and no way to reach that with such heavy seas. These are treacherous waters; we'd crash on the shoreline if we tried to drop anchor." Seeing Emma's disappointment, he added, "Some good comes of every difficulty, William. Ship's boy is not an easy job, but you are learning new skills."

"I am," Emma agreed, "but I'd rather my schooling included decent food and a bed."

For the rest of the morning Emma tried to see the land, but she never did.

The weather had gradually grown warmer as they sailed toward the equator, with high humidity that left Emma mopping her brow.

In late afternoon on the day land was sighted, the temperature suddenly dropped and the wind blew harder. Emma welcomed the cooler air. There had been many rains and three gusty storms since the ship left Liverpool; all had passed in a few hours without any danger.

This time the high winds and rain increased much faster. Within an hour the rain fell in sheets so heavy that Emma could not see from one rail to the other.

Orders flew as thick as the raindrops:

"Boy! Help me here."

"Drop the shutters, boy."

Emma struggled to do as she was told. She was thoroughly soaked by the time she had helped lash down everything on deck and drop the shutters over every porthole. The ship rocked from side to side on the waves. Emma could not keep her balance without holding on to the rail.

Captain Bacon had the crew stretch ropes taut from one side rail to the other. If the giant waves washed over the ship, the men on watch could hold on to the ropes to keep from being swept overboard.

The storm's fury increased. Instead of riding the waves, the ship now bounced from one roller to another, making it even harder for those on deck to keep their balance.

"Get below, boy!" Captain Bacon bellowed at Emma. "Stay in the galley."

Emma, glad to be out of the rain, braced herself against a wall to keep from being thrown about the room as the ship battled the huge waves.

The small table where Cook chopped vegetables slid across the galley floor and bumped into Emma's legs.

A potato, roasted for the meal that Captain Bacon had not had time to eat, rolled across the floor. Emma grabbed it and looked to see if Cook was watching her. He was busy trying to keep the stack of plates from toppling.

Emma stuffed the potato in the pocket of her trousers. It would be a rare treat later when the storm was over and she was alone in her sleeping place.

The ship's bell clanged. *Bong! Bong! Bong!*

"What does that mean?" Emma asked.

"The clapper probably broke loose," Cook answered. "No way to keep it tied in this wind."

The ship leaned sideways; the table moved away from Emma and banged against the cupboard door. Water gushed down the stairway, along the passage, and into the galley. Emma clutched the apple barrel, trying to keep her balance. The water was soon up to her knees.

Years earlier, during summer outings at the lake, Papa had insisted that Emma learn to swim. Emma had liked being able to stay afloat and to propel herself with kicks and strokes. She had never feared the water, but the lake water was smooth and calm, not like this angry sea. For the first time, Emma felt afraid of the water.

The ship listed in the other direction. The barrel tumbled out of her hands and crashed into the opposite wall. Dishes fell from the shelves despite Cook's efforts to keep them in place. The coffeepot toppled, spilling hot coffee into the water.

On the deck above her, voices shouted one on top of another, but the words were blown away before Emma could make them out.

Bang! Crash! Loud noises came from all directions. The potato bin fell over, dumping its contents.

The constant tolling of the bell added a dramatic, unreal quality to the chaos.

The water was waist-high on Emma when Cook jammed a wide-brimmed hat on his head and said, "I'll take my chances on deck." Emma watched him wade out of the galley and climb the stairs.

More water poured into the small room. Emma did not want to disobey Captain Bacon's orders to stay in the galley, but she feared she would drown if she remained there much longer.

She pushed through the water to the stairs and pulled herself up by the handrail as the rushing sea water tried to shove her back down. As she mounted the steps, the water behind her deepened, climbing the walls of the galley and passageway.

Above her she saw Captain Bacon and Mr. Yule. Both wore yellow oilskins. They wrestled desperately with the wheel, trying to keep the ship upright.

"Hold it steady!" Captain Bacon cried, even as the wheel spun loosely in his grasp.

Emma was nearly to the top when a sudden sharp noise, different from the others, rose above the howling wind and the shouts of the sailors. *Crack! Snap!* The sound of splintering wood filled Emma with fresh fear.

A voice burst through the torrent.

"Man overboard!"

Terrified, Emma gripped the railing.

"Man overboard!" The shout came again, a different voice this time. Had more than one sailor been swept into the raging sea?

Emma made it up to the deck just as an even worse cry rang out.

"We're going down!"

"We're going down!"

CHAPTER

8

CAPTAIN BACON BELLOWED, "Man your stations!" But Emma saw many crewmen abandon their posts and rush to the side of the ship.

The wooden steps beneath Emma's feet shuddered for an instant as she clung to the handrail, horrified. Then the cracking sound repeated and Emma was thrown backward.

She landed in water, and more water swept over her.

The wind tore a wooden hatch cover loose from the deck and flung it down the stairs toward Emma. The hatch cover clunked against the wall, then floated in the passageway.

Choking, Emma struggled to the surface of the water. Her hands, groping for the rail, found the edge of the hatch cover. Holding on to it, she pulled herself up until her head was above water.

She realized that the hatch cover could serve as a liferaft, so she climbed on top of it and lay facedown, gripping the edges.

The water rose rapidly, filling the entire passageway and pushing the hatch cover back up the stairwell. She now floated near Mr. Yule, who stood knee-deep in water, clinging desperately to the wheel.

Another sharp *crack* exploded; it seemed to come from above and below and all sides at once. The tallest mast fell sideways as if it had been sawed in half. It shattered the ship's railing when it landed.

The wind-blown rain and the mighty waves merged into a wall of water crashing down on the *Black Lightning*.

Through it all, the bell continued to clang.

A jagged bolt of lightning cut through the dark clouds, followed instantly by a loud clap of thunder. An enormous rolling wave approached the ship, rising higher and higher as it came.

Just before the roller hit, Emma closed her eyes and held her breath. She put her face on the hatch cover, clinging to the edges to keep from being swept off.

Water poured over her.

The hatch cover surged forward, blasting through the screams of the sailors and away from the terrible snapping noises of the doomed ship.

When she opened her eyes, she was no longer aboard the *Black Lightning*. She was still lying on the hatch cover, but she was fifty feet away from the ship. The cover rose high in the air as the waves roared upward, then plummeted with their descent.

Only one end of the *Black Lightning* remained above the surface. Emma saw crewmen clinging to the jib boom, which now pointed straight up. One by one they jumped off as the boom, too, slowly sank into the sea.

The bell was silent.

Pieces of wood littered the churning surface of the sea around her along with torn sails and the crew's personal belongings. Emma shook with cold and dread; her teeth chattered as the wind buffeted the hatch cover she rode.

She saw people swimming but couldn't make out who they were. She wondered if they could possibly make it to shore.

Voices came from the surging sea:

"Help! Help!"

"God have mercy!"

Emma heard the cries but could not see where they came from. The calls fell like raindrops into the ocean and disappeared.

How far were they from land? Were any ships nearby?

How long would her hatch cover stay afloat? Could she possibly stay on it until she was sighted and rescued?

Oh, Papa, she thought, I should have stayed with Aunt Martha and Odolf. No matter how dreadful Odolf was to me, at least I would be alive.

Night fell. With the moon obscured by clouds, Emma could no longer see survivors in the water or the broken remains of the ship.

The rain stopped.

The calls for help ceased. Emma heard only the wind and the rumbling ocean.

Wave after wave hoisted Emma high into the darkness, and plunged her back to the raging sea. Trembling, she clung to the hatch cover and prayed for help.

During the night, the storm wore itself out. The wind diminished, the waves grew calmer, and the sun rose in a golden glow to dry Emma's hair and clothing.

Steam rose from the hatch cover. The ocean stretched away in all directions. Debris from the *Black Lightning* still floated on the surface, but the pieces were more scattered now.

She saw no one swimming and no one clinging to pieces of wreckage.

Is it possible, she wondered, that I am the only survivor? She thought of Cook and Mr. Yule, of Captain Bacon and of Maury, the sailor who had taught her the names of the stars. Were all of them buried beneath the water? Even though their mission of transporting and selling slaves was an evil one, it grieved Emma to think they were gone. Especially Maury.

Emma's empty stomach growled. She reached in her pocket for the potato, but hours of being soaked with sea water had turned it into a soggy, mushy mess. She scooped the pulp into her fingers, dismayed by the small amount, and put it in her mouth.

She had barely swallowed when she realized it was a mistake to eat the potato mush. It had done little to ease her hunger and, soaked as it was with the salty sea water, it had increased her thirst.

She had no food, no fresh water, and no way to summon help. All she could do was float on the hatch cover and hope another ship came close enough to spot her.

Too exhausted to think, Emma closed her eyes and let the ocean rock her to sleep.

She dozed and woke for two more days and nights. Each hour she was awake seemed to last ten hours until she felt as if she had been floating alone for half a lifetime.

By the third morning she was weak from hunger and nearly delirious with thirst. The hot humid air made her sweat, robbing her body of moisture.

Blisters rose on her sunburned face and hands; painful cracks split her lips. Even her eyeballs ached from sunburn.

Emma stared into the vast, rolling sea. Maybe the sailors were luckier than I, she thought. For them it was over quickly.

She was tempted to let herself roll off the cover into the endless ocean and put an end to her misery. It would be easier than clinging to it any longer.

Yet she stayed on the cover, not willing to give up. If I sink into the sea, she decided, it will not be by choice.

Midafternoon on the third day, black clouds covered the sun. Drops of rain splashed down. Emma lay on her back with her eyes closed and her mouth open, trying to catch as many raindrops as possible. She wished she had Mattie's rain barrel.

The wind rose, the waves surged higher, and the drops became a steady rain.

Emma welcomed the downpour. She sat up, cupped her hands, and gratefully swallowed as much water as she could catch. Besides easing the pain of the sunburn, the water cleared her mind.

Soon torrents of rain pelted her. A giant roller picked up the hatch cover, lifted it high, and carried it hundreds of feet forward. Emma had to lie down again to avoid falling off. She wondered if she had enough strength left to hold fast to the hatch cover as she had during the first storm.

She rolled onto her stomach and gripped the rim. Another roller followed, and another. These waves were different from the ones Emma had ridden during the last storm. They were high and long and powerful, but they were also more sustained, as if they had a destination. The wind was at her back, pushing the waves forward.

The wind and rain eased after two hours, but the sun did not return.

The waves continued to carry Emma in long, sweeping arcs. She lifted her head and saw, far ahead, a thin dark line across the horizon.

She squinted at the line. Was it more dark clouds, bringing another storm? Or could it possibly be land?

CHAPTER

9

—⟨⟨⟨⟩⟩⟩—

Each wave carried Emma closer to the line in the distance.

She rose to her knees, staring ahead through the mist. The line became darker and more uneven until finally Emma could see that it was a row of trees.

She saw no other ships and no sign of buildings or people on the shore. The waves rose high, each one carrying her as far upward as it did forward.

Hurry! she thought. She put her arms into the water and paddled, trying to make the hatch cover move more quickly toward land.

Soon she could make out individual trees and other vegetation, most of it unlike anything she had seen before. Since the *Black Lightning* had been about halfway through its journey when it sank, Emma knew she must be approaching the western coast of central Africa. Near the equator, Maury had said.

As the waves carried her closer, she saw that there was no beach. A tangle of trees came right to the water's edge, hiding whatever lay farther inland. The biggest waves rose above the tree-tops and crashed down on them, washing through the leaves and branches and eroding the soil near the roots.

Fearing that her hatch cover might be lifted up and dumped into the trees, Emma slid off it and swam toward shore. The waves continued to push her in the right direction. Excitement gave strength to her tired body as she kicked her feet and flung her arms forward.

The sea water stung her eyes as she tried to see how to get ashore.

Emma splashed forward until her outstretched hands touched dirt. Digging her fingers into the damp soil, she scrambled on to the land and collapsed. Long, rolling waves crashed rhythmically against an exposed tree root near Emma's feet.

One giant wave poured over her. Emma scrambled to her feet and clung to a tree trunk until it passed. She had thought Africa was mostly desert, but this looked more like a forest. Trees of all sizes grew along the coastline as far as she could see. They were strange trees, with tangled thickets between them. What was the word Maury had used? *Jungle.*

Hoping to see a ship, she scanned the ocean behind her one last time. She saw only her hatch cover, bobbing on a wave.

The jungle appeared impenetrable, but she knew she must search for food and fresh water.

Emma pushed through a mass of small bushes and headed inland. A giant tree with vines dangling from its branches seemed to grow out of bare rock. Emma skirted it, peering anxiously at the vines, which looked far too much like snakes.

The huge trees provided both shade and moisture. It was not raining, yet water dripped from leaves and vines; the ground underfoot was damp.

A fallen tree rotted on the ground ahead of her. As she stepped over it, she saw that water had collected in small hollows along the tree trunk.

Emma knelt beside the tree, put her lips to the crumbling bark, and sucked the water into her mouth. There wasn't much—only two or three tablespoons in each hollow—but she drained them all, and the lukewarm liquid tasted better than any hot tea Emma had ever sipped.

The small pools of water gave her hope. If she could find water, she would survive. She would locate berries or nuts or some kind of edible plant, and she would live here in the jungle until another ship sailed down the coast. Then Emma would send a signal and be rescued.

Encouraged, she continued deeper into the jungle. Giant roots fanned out from the base of trees; many roots were as high as Emma's shoulders. On some of the trees the exposed roots were decaying. She wondered why the roots stayed on top of the soil rather than going down into the earth.

She listened intently, anticipating animal sounds, as she moved slowly through the thicket. Emma's clothes clung to her skin in the warm dampness. Sweat ran down the sides of her face. She worried that she could never find enough water to replace what her body was losing. She removed Odolf's shirt and tied it around her waist. Her chemise was almost as dirty as the shirt; Mattie would scold, if she were there.

Emma's stomach contracted in painful spasms. She had never known true hunger before. Even on board the *Black Lightning*, where the food was both sparse and unappetizing, she had always found something to eat. For weeks she had resented the cold beans and bitter coffee that Cook called breakfast; now she would welcome such a meal.

Palmlike plants lifted their leaves high above Emma's head. She pushed through them, trying not to trip on the smaller plants and stunted trees that grew in no particular pattern on the jungle floor.

Fan-shaped leaves spread over her head like a group of green umbrellas so that she saw only glimpses of the gray sky. Although she knew it was still midday, the dim light that filtered through the leaves made it seem like dusk.

In some places trees of varying heights made layers of leaves so that only the tallest ever had sunlight. Deep shadows shaded the ground in those areas, making it almost completely dark. Woody vines looped around tree trunks, climbing toward the light.

Water dripped from the canopy of leaves above her down to the ferns at her ankles. Emma cupped one hand, held it at the tip of a large leaf, and used her other hand to direct the drops of water into her palm. Then she licked her palm. She continued from leaf to leaf, collecting a small amount of moisture from each. She found a tiny pool of water trapped in a hollow stump and drank that, too.

As she straightened, a flock of parrots chattered their disapproval. Emma jumped at the sound, then smiled when she saw the source. The parrots' bright orange wings were colorful against the green trees as the birds flapped noisily away.

Emma suddenly sank up to her ankles in a rotting tree trunk. Large black beetles scurried away from her feet. Emma wondered if the beetles might be edible. She looked around for something to use as a weapon, to kill one of them.

At the same time she imagined putting a squashed beetle in her mouth. Gagging at the thought, Emma decided to try awhile longer to find berries or nuts. She would give anything for a pan of Mattie's hot biscuits or a big serving of Yorkshire pudding.

She plucked a large leaf from a tree and bit into it. Then she put the whole leaf in her mouth, and chewed. Surely there is some nourishment in leaves, she thought. Although the leaf had no flavor, it was far more appetizing than a raw beetle.

A thick mist floated down through the trees; Emma felt as if she were walking into a cloud. She could see only a few feet in front of her. Minutes later rain poured down, dripping through the tiers of leaves.

Emma came to a small clearing where water gushed down a shallow gully. She knelt beside the stream and drank her fill. She splashed the fresh water over her face and hair, wishing she had a bit of soap.

Her hunger pangs eased. Water in her stomach was better than nothing.

I need to mark this spot, Emma thought, so that I can return here for water. She tore a strip of material from the bottom of Odolf's shirt, and tied it at eye level around the branch of a tree. She continued through the jungle, tying another piece of shirt to a branch whenever the last one was nearly out of sight.

Her wet shoes chafed her heels, causing raw spots on them.

The rain passed as quickly as it had begun. The tree leaves whispered above her; birds twittered nearby. With her thirst abated, Emma continued her search for food.

As she pushed through the jungle, she heard a new sound.

"Hoot." An animal's call, low and ominous, came from somewhere in the trees.

Emma stood still, every nerve alert.

"Hoot." The call repeated and this time it was answered by a "Hoot!" that came from over her head.

Emma looked up into the nearest tree. About thirty feet above her, she saw a large nest that had been made by twisting small leafy branches into a rounded shape. As she watched, a huge arm covered with thick black hair reached out of the nest. A hand with long, gnarled fingers and a small thumb grasped the branch that the nest sat on.

Emma held her breath and watched.

A chimpanzee, larger than Emma, raised his head from the leafy nest and looked down.

When he spotted Emma, his massive shoulders and thick chest rose quickly from the nest, followed by the rest of his powerful-looking body. Coarse fur covered everything except his hands, feet, face, and ears. He had no tail.

The immense black beast stared at Emma. She stood at the base of the tree, too frightened to move, and stared back at him.

Chapter

10

―◦◦◦―

EMMA WANTED TO run, but she feared the chimp would pursue her.

The animal, asleep in the tree, had not heard Emma approach. Now, awakened by the call of another chimp, he seemed as surprised to see Emma as Emma was to see him. His bright brown eyes watched her warily.

"Hoot," the chimp said again.

She thought of saying *hoot* back, but the sound did not seem to be a greeting. It was more of a warning call.

Emma wondered how many other chimpanzees were nearby. Better to be quiet, she decided, though she felt the chimp might hear her heart thumping in her chest.

He gazed at her for a few more seconds before

launching himself into the air. His long arms reached out to grasp a limb on the next tree. Going hand over hand through the treetops, he swung quickly out of Emma's sight.

Emma took a deep breath, trying to calm herself. She thought the chimpanzee was a good sign; it meant food must be nearby.

Although she feared the chimpanzee, she felt instinctively that because the animal looked so much like a human, she could eat whatever he ate.

Hoping the chimp would lead her to food, she walked in the direction he had gone, moving as quietly as possible. It was hard to follow directly after him because the chimp could swing in a straight line while Emma had to skirt thickets and sidestep large tree trunks.

She came to a partial meadow, an open area with fewer trees. Waist-high grass, most of it with edges as sharp as swords, slowed her progress. She put Odolf's shirt back on to protect her arms from the razorlike blades, and realized she had forgotten to rip more strips of cloth to mark the trail back to the gully.

On the far side of the meadow she thought she saw movement high in the branches of the trees. She eased forward cautiously, hoping that the chimp had led her to edible fruit.

A breeze blew toward her, cooling her face and shoulders, but she didn't think the motion in the trees was caused only by the wind.

Looking up at the treetops ahead, she failed to see a bull buffalo sleeping in a patch of grass. Emma stepped through the high grass, stubbed her toe on the dozing beast, and stumbled backward.

"Oh!" she said as she struggled to regain her balance.

The startled buffalo lumbered to his feet and turned to look at Emma. Large horns curved down the sides of his wide face and then curved up again. His ears stuck out sideways below the horns, and his tail switched from side to side of his enormous body.

Emma took a step backward. She hoped if she did not threaten the animal, he would stand still and watch her leave.

Instead the buffalo lowered his horns toward Emma.

She continued to back away, moving as quickly as she could.

The buffalo pawed the ground with his front hooves.

He's going to charge me! Emma thought.

Fear energized her weary body. Emma spun around and fled back toward the trees.

Behind her the buffalo snorted. Then she heard hooves thudding after her.

A large tree at the edge of the clearing seemed her best hope for escape. Emma raced toward it.

The buffalo ran faster than she did; she could hear it coming closer.

The sharp grass slashed at her as she pushed her way through it. As she reached the tree, she felt the buffalo's heavy warm breath behind her. He was only inches away.

Emma grabbed one of the vines that twined around the tree trunk and pulled herself up. As her foot reached the vine, the buffalo's horns slammed into the trunk. One horn barely missed her ankle.

Emma stretched her other arm over her head, grasped the vine higher up, and continued to climb.

The enraged buffalo, fully awake now, jabbed at the tree trunk with his horns. The tree shuddered from the blows; the branch Emma clung to dropped some of its leaves.

Emma looked down at the shaggy brown beast with his broad nose and massive body, and knew she was lucky to be alive. If the buffalo had not been sleeping soundly when Emma stumbled upon him, she would have been gored immediately.

And if she had not strengthened her muscles by her hard work on board the *Black Lightning*, she would not have been strong enough to hoist herself up into the tree so quickly.

Perhaps Maury was right, Emma thought. Perhaps some good does come from every difficulty. Climbing to the top of the mast and hauling heavy rigging had prepared her to climb this tree in a hurry.

She wondered what good might come from being treed by an angry buffalo.

The buffalo butted the tree for another five minutes and then seemed to realize his efforts were futile. He gave one last, angry snort and then headed back toward the meadow.

Emma watched him disappear into the tall grass. She remained in the tree long after he left, making sure the buffalo was far enough away that he would not hear or smell her when she got down. She wondered why he had not smelled her as she approached him in the grass and decided it was because the breeze had blown her scent away from him.

She peered around at the nearby trees and plants. The jungle looked different from high in a tree.

One tree trunk behind her was particularly interesting. A network of roots went all the way up the trunk to the branches, forming a twisted pattern on the outside of the bark. Emma's eyes followed the tangle of clinging roots up to the top—and saw green clumps hanging like ornaments.

Emma licked her lips. Each round, green fruit was ridged and came to a tapered point at its stem. Figs. She was almost certain she was looking at a fig tree.

She lowered herself carefully from her perch, listening often to be sure the buffalo was not returning. When her feet touched the ground, she hurried to the tree she had spotted and started up it.

It was more difficult to climb than the first tree, for the shallow roots that wound around the trunk did not provide much space on which to rest her feet. But Emma's fingers clung to the roots and she managed to pull herself up to the lowest branch. From there, she reached out and plucked one of the green fruits.

What if it isn't a fig? she thought. What if it's poisonous?

Hunger overcame her doubt and she bit into the fruit. Because of the green color she had assumed the fruit was not yet ripe, and she expected the flesh to be firm. Instead it was soft and sweet.

Emma ate quickly and then picked another. Nothing—not even her favorite birthday meal of roast lamb and rice pudding or a bowl of Aunt Martha's raspberry fool—had ever tasted so good.

She ate the second fig more slowly, chewing it well and savoring each mouthful.

Emma ate seven of the figs and then, still hungry, made herself wait awhile before eating more. After so many days without food, she feared she would be sick if she ate too much at once.

While she sat in the fig tree, waiting for her stomach to digest the feast, she felt excited and optimistic. She had found water; she had found food. If she was careful not to arouse any more wild animals, she thought she could survive here in the African jungle.

She began to make a plan. She decided not to go back to the meadow. It was too unprotected. She would stay in this part of the jungle, near the coast, so that she could go to the ocean several times a day to see if any ships were sailing past.

She hoped to spot a ship sailing north, and imagined getting picked up and taken back to England.

England. A flood of memories washed over Emma: Mama humming happy songs as she tied rags in Emma's damp hair to make it curl; Mattie in the kitchen, sneaking Emma crisp bites of roast (Emma preferred the end cut) before it was time to serve; Papa in his dark coat and top hat, arriving home and greeting Mama with a smile.

They probably thought she was dead. Even if the *Wayfarer* had sailed before they got word that Emma was missing, they would know by now. She hoped the worry had not worsened Mama's condition. She hoped Mama was feeling better.

Emma imagined Odolf's expression when she finally returned and told him that she had been a ship's boy and had survived a wreck at sea, and had lived alone in an African jungle. He would probably accuse her of making up the whole story.

Remembering how Odolf had bent her arm behind her, Emma clenched her fist. I'm stronger than I used to be, she thought. Just let him try to bend my arm now; I'll give him a dose of his own medicine.

She ate several more figs. The dim light in the jungle grew fainter; soon it would be dark. Even if night were not approaching, Emma knew she needed sleep. The days spent riding the ocean on the hatch cover without food or water had exhausted her.

She wondered where she should spend the night. The chimpanzee had made a nest in the tree, but Emma feared she would fall out if she tried to do that.

Moisture dripped constantly in the damp jungle. She knew she could not sleep unless she was protected from it.

She climbed down the fig tree and walked slowly, searching for a dry place.

Something white through the trees caught her eye. When she looked closer, she saw it was one of the pieces of cloth she had tied to a tree earlier. Good, Emma thought. That means I'm still near the place where I found water.

She followed her flags and found the gully again, but the water in it was only a trickle. Emma concluded that the stream flowed only when it rained and vowed to return at the first sign of a storm.

She decided to build a shelter near her source of water and live there until she was rescued.

She saw three large trees growing close together, almost in a straight line. They will be one side of my shelter, Emma decided. She pulled small shrubs, vines, and spindly saplings away from the trio of trees, clearing a space at their base.

She broke nine branches, each about an inch in diameter, from nearby young trees and angled them against the three large tree trunks.

Next Emma looked for the biggest leaves she could find. She saw the trees that had reminded her of umbrellas. Long slender stems attached the large leaves to the tree trunk, making the leaves easy to pick.

Feeling more and more confident as a climber, Emma shinnied up the tree until she could reach the leaves. She plucked dozens of them and let them flutter to the jungle floor.

Back on the ground, she laid the leaves on top of the angled branches, overlapping them to form a roof. She wanted more of the big leaves to use as a mattress but she was too weary to climb the tree again. Instead she gathered smaller leaves that she could reach from the ground and piled them under the roof she had fashioned.

By then it was almost completely dark. She checked around her shelter for ants, snakes, beetles or anything else that might crawl on her while she slept. Finding no creatures, she crept in to her shelter and lay on the leaves.

The jungle cooled quickly; she put Odolf's

shirt on again. Tomorrow she would gather more large leaves to use as a blanket.

For the first time since her last night on the *Black Lightning* Emma said her bedtime prayers. For years Mama stood beside Emma's bed at night to hear Emma recite her evening prayer. "Blessings bring to Mama and Papa," Emma murmured. "Blessings bring to Mattie and Uncle Edward."

Her prayer offered, Emma lay listening to the sounds of the African night. High above her, the treetops whispered secrets. Water dripped softly on her roof. Her bed had a dank, pungent smell.

Mosquitoes buzzed around her head. Twice Emma smashed one against her cheek and had to wipe blood from her fingers. She feared she would be bitten during the night, and had no way to prevent it.

A soft rustling made her stiffen in panic. Emma held her breath as a small animal scurried past the entry to her shelter. She could not see it, but she heard its movement as it passed.

Emma tried to guess what the animal might have been, but her imagination failed her. The only African animals she could think of were elephants and giraffes, but this had been a small creature, probably the size of a rat.

No, not a rat, she told herself. She did not want to think about rats scuttling around in the night. This creature, she decided, was the size of a kitten. A sweet soft kitten.

She wished she had a book about Africa. Knowledge of the jungle would make her less afraid, but she had no way to gain that knowledge except by experience.

Wondering what tomorrow would bring, Emma closed her eyes and drifted into an uneasy sleep.

CHAPTER

11

—⟨ഗ⟩—

A snapping sound woke her. Emma knew immediately that the sound had been a small branch breaking. Apprehension tingled down her arms. She lay still, listening.

The daylight surprised Emma. She had expected to wake often in the night; instead, she had slept soundly.

The snapping sound continued; something was moving through the underbrush not far from her shelter. An image of the enraged buffalo flashed through her mind. Had he returned, looking for her?

I need a weapon, Emma thought. Instead of filling my pocket with a potato, I should have taken a galley knife or Cook's pistol.

Emma carefully rolled on to her belly, hoping

that whatever creature was close would not hear her move. She raised up on her elbows so she could see out one end of her shelter.

A large chimpanzee ambled into view and sat down next to a mound of reddish clay. He looked like the same chimp Emma had seen in the tree nest, though she couldn't be sure.

The clay mound came nearly to the seated chimp's chin. It reminded Emma of the sand structures she had made at the lake shore when she was small. She used to pile the damp sand as high as she could and pat it firmly to make it stay in place. She was always unhappy when rain, or other children, destroyed her creations.

The chimp broke a foot-long section of vine from a tree. He stripped the leaves from the vine and then put one end of the vine in his mouth and bit off a small piece. Emma thought he was going to eat the vine, but he spit the piece out and then pushed that end of the vine into the mound of clay.

He soon withdrew the vine and picked something off it with his lips. He put the vine back into the clay, pulled it out, and again ate something off it.

Emma watched the chimp repeat this process over and over. Occasionally he dug in the dirt mound with his fingers, apparently to open a new hole for his piece of vine.

He's fishing for some sort of insect, Emma decided. He made a little tool from the vine, and when he puts it in the mound, whatever is in there must hang on to the vine while he pulls it out. The chimpanzee eats his catch and repeats the process.

Emma didn't know what insect lived in mounds of clay. Ants, perhaps? Or beetles like the ones she had seen yesterday?

As she watched, Emma's fear of the chimp lessened. He looked much like a human as he bent over to probe the openings. His wide lips curved upward in a smile, and when he concentrated on his work, he appeared calm and not at all threatening.

Twice the chimp put his nose to the clay and sniffed it. Emma wondered if he could smell where the insects were inside the mound.

The chimp continued to poke patiently at the mound of clay for nearly an hour. Then he dropped the piece of vine and walked away.

Emma inched forward in order to see where he went, but she quickly lost sight of him.

The sides of her neck itched and so did her hands. Emma saw small red welts on the backs of her hands and knew the mosquitoes had found her while she slept.

A few minutes after the chimp left, she crawled out of her shelter and went to the clay mound. Emma saw small insects busily patching the holes that the chimp had made. They were the size of large ants, but light colored, and their bodies were not segmented.

The insects looked like the ones that had destroyed one corner of Papa's carriage house the summer before. Emma thought the mound was a termite nest. With so much rotting wood on the jungle floor, the termites would have plenty to eat.

Emma poked the chimp's piece of vine into one of the holes, waited a few seconds, and withdrew it. Four termites clung to the vine.

They're edible, she told herself, *and I'm hungry.* Before she could change her mind, she stuck the end of the vine in her mouth and sucked the termites off, quickly smashing them with her tongue against the roof of her mouth.

The termites were bland, with hardly any flavor at all.

Emma swallowed, astonished at what she had just done. She who always refused to eat rare roast beef because it looked too bloody, and who screamed and called for Papa whenever she found a spider in the house, had just consumed four live termites.

Mattie will never believe it, Emma thought. She giggled, thinking of Mattie's reaction.

She wondered why the chimp would work so hard for such a small amount of tasteless food. In the hour that he had jabbed his vine into the mound, the chimp had probably eaten less than half a cup of termites.

Maybe they're a delicacy, she thought. Maybe the chimps eat termites for dessert.

"Hoot." The sound came from behind her.

Emma's smile disappeared.

Three chimps, partially hidden by a tangle of vines and small trees, peered at her. Their fur stood out the way a cat's fur stands on end when it is angry or frightened, making the chimps look twice as big as they really were.

She wondered if the chimps were angry at her for taking their food.

"Hoot."

I'll put the vine down and walk away from the mound of clay, Emma decided. I'll show them that I won't eat any more of their termites.

Emma dropped the piece of vine back in the dirt and started to stand up. As soon as she moved the chimps barked a frightened-sounding bark and ran away.

They seem more scared of me than I am of them, Emma thought. If they had wanted to attack, they could have done so before I ever noticed them.

Emma looked carefully around for other animals. Seeing none, she returned to the fig tree, climbed it, and ate her fill.

Then she made her way to the edge of the ocean, near the spot where she had come ashore. The deep blue water stretched as far as she could see, melding in the distance with the lighter blue sky. The rolling waves followed one another to land and then retreated again.

Although she watched for nearly an hour, she

saw no ship, nor did she see the hatch cover that had served as her life raft. She wished she had brought it ashore with her, rather than abandoning it. It would have made a sturdy side for her shelter.

It's too late to change that now, Emma thought. It's too late to change a lot of things.

She went back into the jungle to search for food.

It rained every day, sometimes more than once. Each morning Emma drank from hollows in logs, and whenever it rained hard she returned to the gully where the small stream temporarily flowed.

On her fifth day in the jungle, Emma searched for thin flexible vines. She wove them into a basket, pulling the vines tightly together so there were no air spaces. She lined the basket with layers of overlapping leaves.

That afternoon, when it rained hard enough for water to wash through the gully, she filled her basket with water and put it in her shelter.

She continued to drink from the hollows in fallen logs, but the basket of water eased her worry that she would not be able to find enough to drink. She often drank from it at night, and she refilled it each time the stream ran down the gully.

Emma found more fig trees and grew adept at climbing them, pulling herself up quickly and wrapping her legs around the branches to keep her balance so she could pick fruit with both hands.

She practiced climbing other trees, too, just in case she needed to escape from another buffalo.

She found more termite mounds and forced herself to eat more of the tasteless insects. As soon as she got them in her mouth, she closed her eyes and pinched her nose shut while she swallowed. It seemed easier to eat termites if she couldn't see or smell.

Mama had always told Emma that she needed a variety of food in order to be healthy. Maybe termites were full of necessary nutrients. She also ate an assortment of leaves, chewing them thoroughly to make them more digestible.

The mosquitoes continued to be a problem, especially at night. Emma slept in Odolf's long-sleeved shirt, but she frequently woke with bites on her face and hands.

She saw the chimps often. Although they always ran away from her, she followed and watched them whenever she could, hoping they would lead her to other sources of food. The fig crop would soon be gone, and Emma knew she could not survive on leaves and insects.

Emma especially enjoyed watching a baby chimp. The adult chimps had black faces and ears but the baby's face and ears were light colored, and he had a fluff of white fur for a tail. The baby sat on his mother's lap and climbed on his mother's shoulders just as a human infant does. Sometimes he played with stones or twigs.

One afternoon Emma saw the mother chimp fishing for termites. The baby did not fish, nor did the mother offer him any of the insects. But the baby watched closely, observing everything the mother did as if he were taking lessons.

In the middle of their fishing lesson, a sudden cloudburst dumped buckets of rain. The mother chimp pulled the baby close against her stomach, wrapped her arms around him, and hunched over to shield him from the rain.

When the storm passed, water still streamed from the mother chimp's coarse fur, but the baby emerged dry from his snug haven. The mother chimp plucked a handful of leaves from a tree and used them like a towel to dry herself.

By then Emma knew this part of the jungle as well as she knew her own home in England. She recognized individual trees, stumps, and rotting logs. She knew where to go after a rain shower to drink pools of collected water.

As soon as she awoke each morning, she walked to the shore and stood looking out to sea. She returned in midday and again at dusk. Day after day, she saw only the endless waves.

What if a ship passes when I'm asleep? Emma worried. The *Black Lightning* had sailed at night. A ship could pass in the darkness, and I would have no way of knowing it was there.

CHAPTER

12

━━◖◗◖◗━━

ONE MORNING EMMA was awakened by thunder. When she looked out the opening of her shelter, she saw streaks of lightning through the trees.

More thunder boomed. Rain soon followed, pelting her makeshift roof so hard that some of the leaves gave way, and the water dripped through.

Her water basket was empty. She knew the gully would be gushing with rain water now, so she took the basket and headed in that direction.

Just before she reached the gully, she heard loud hooting sounds from the hillside ahead. She could tell it was a group of chimps, but she had never heard them yell so loudly before.

Emma went forward carefully, staying behind trees until she could see where the chimps were.

Ahead on the hillside, she saw a dozen or more huge male chimpanzees. One of them raced down the hill by leaning on his hands and swinging his legs under his body from behind. He repeated the motion, hooting loudly.

At the bottom of the hill he broke a branch from a tree, whacked it on the ground, and then dragged it along behind him. Still hooting, he climbed a different tree and swung wildly through the branches.

The other chimps yelled and jumped about as they watched. Another chimp rushed down the hill upright, straight toward a tree. When he got to the tree, he put one hand on the trunk and whirled around it.

Lightning split the coal-colored clouds. Thunder rumbled in the distance, and the wind whipped the rain sideways.

As yet another chimp stormed down the hill, the one who had run down first dropped his branch and plodded back up again on all fours to repeat the charge.

Emma saw the mother chimp and her baby watching the activity from the top of the hill. It surprised Emma that the baby was not tucked away from the storm; apparently the mother chimp was too interested in the crazed hooting and wild antics of the male chimps to remember to keep her baby dry.

Rainwater poured down the gully, but Emma could not get to it without being seen by the chimps. In their excited condition, she did not know if they would run from her as usual. She couldn't take the chance of startling them when they were already so agitated. She stayed hidden and watched.

Jagged spears of lightning streaked through the sky. Thunder followed the lightning, closer now, so loud it seemed to shake the earth.

Several chimps plummeted down the hill at the same time. The hooting grew louder, and the chimps became more frenzied. One tree rocked from side to side as two of the huge chimps climbed it at the same time.

All at once the few chimps still at the top of the hill charged down to join the others. One of them ripped a large branch from a tree and then flailed the tree with it.

Rain pounded down so fast that the jungle floor could not soak it up. The stream that flowed down the gully suddenly became a violent river.

All of the male chimps were at the bottom of the hill when the stream overflowed its channel. A torrent of water washed over the crest of the hill and plunged downward, tearing saplings up by the roots.

The chimps, hooting wildly, ran away from the churning flood. Emma heard their excited cries long after they disappeared from her sight.

The mother chimp, intent on the actions of the males, was caught off guard when the stream turned into a raging river. By the time she realized that the males were running away, it was too late for her to escape the water that cascaded toward her.

The flooding stream caught her from behind, knocking her off her feet. Water flowed over her head as she fell, facedown.

As Emma watched in horror, the baby chimp was ripped from his mother's grasp and swept away.

The mother struggled to her feet and scrambled out of the water's path. Screaming, she ran downhill along the edge of the water, reaching out desperately for her baby.

By then the river had become too wide for her to touch the baby, and too deep and powerful for him to stand.

The little chimp tumbled over and over in the water. His small hands flailed above his head, but either he did not know how to swim, or the current was too strong.

Emma raced from her hiding place. She grabbed the large branch that the male chimp had dragged along the ground. She ran to the edge of the water as the baby chimp came closer.

The mother chimp hesitated when she saw Emma, then continued to run along the edge of the water toward Emma, trying to grab her baby.

The water streamed down Emma's face so hard that it was difficult to see. As the baby chimp approached, Emma extended the end of the branch, holding it just over the top of the water.

She waited until the little chimp was almost to the branch. Then Emma plunged the branch down into the water where the chimp bumped into it.

Grab it! she thought. *Please, please grab it and hold on.*

Emma felt the branch jerk as the baby chimp's fingers closed around it. Emma gripped her end of the branch as hard as she could to keep the river from pulling it out of her hands.

The water continued to push the baby downstream, but he put his other hand around the branch, too, and did not let go.

Emma braced her feet and pulled with all her strength on the end of the branch. Her arms ached as she struggled to haul the little chimp out of the river.

The mother chimp jumped up and down beside her, making loud excited noises. Then, as if realizing what Emma was trying to do, the mother chimp stretched both long arms forward and grabbed the branch, too. She gave a mighty tug. The baby chimp skimmed across the surface of the water to the edge and leaped free of the river.

Emma had been pulling so hard that when the baby jumped out of the water and dropped the branch, Emma fell over backward.

The mother chimp gathered her baby into her arms. She examined him quickly, brushing water from his fur with one hand. Then she stood beside Emma, looking down at her.

Emma, unafraid, sat up. Joyous that the baby was all right, she smiled at the two chimps. The mother chimp gazed at Emma for several seconds, then carried her baby off in the direction the male chimps had gone.

After resting for a few minutes, Emma filled her basket with water and put it in her shelter. She didn't go in herself. She was already so drenched there was no point in taking cover, and she didn't want to drip all over her sleeping area.

She thought about breakfast, but she had no appetite. Usually she felt half starved when she woke up; today her stomach was unsettled. Small wonder, she thought, when I eat raw termites, too many figs, and the leaves from unknown plants.

The struggle to rescue the baby chimp had drained Emma of her strength. She felt tired—tired of wearing dirty clothes, tired of always being alert for wild animals, tired of being hungry and having no proper food. Most of all, she was tired of being alone in this wilderness.

I want to go home, Emma thought. I want Mama to wash my hair and tie it with ribbons. I want to read my lessons to her and have her nod her approval. I want to watch Mattie knead the bread dough and put it on the hearth to rise.

A jagged spear of lightning crackled down and split a thick palm tree in two. One half remained standing; the other half fell to the ground with a loud *thunk* only a few yards from where Emma stood.

As the booming thunder surrounded her, tears mixed with the rain that ran down her cheeks. She had thought nothing could be worse than living with Odolf, but she had been wrong.

CHAPTER

13

IGNORING THE RAIN, Emma walked to the ocean to look for ships. The *Black Lightning* had washed toward shore in exactly this kind of storm. Maybe some other ship would be blown off course in this direction, too, and would come close enough to land to see her.

Waves as tall as the fig trees and hundreds of feet wide crested and rolled toward land. Thick spray rose high in the air when the waves crashed against the shore.

Emma stayed back from the edge. She looked out across the rows of whitecaps and froze in surprise. Was that a ship on the horizon, far to her right? It looked no larger than a toy.

She put her hands across her forehead, shielding her eyes from the rain. She squinted at the dark object that rose and fell on the surging waves.

Yes! Emma thought as exhilaration vibrated down her arms. It is a ship! And the wind and waves from the storm will carry it this way.

Still feeling slightly sick to her stomach, she sat down to wait, keeping her eyes fixed on the far-off ship.

After she watched it for half an hour, it appeared larger than when she had first seen it, and she knew it was closer to shore. It had also moved gradually to her left.

The thunder and lightning stopped. The rain eased.

I need a signal, Emma thought. She wished she had a way to start a fire, but there wasn't a dry stick in the entire jungle.

Emma could see the ship clearly now, silhouetted against the sky. She could not make out the figures of those on board, but soon after the rain stopped, she saw the white sails go up.

They'll never see me if I just sit here, Emma thought. I need to do something to attract their attention.

She broke a long limb from a tree and stripped the small branches and leaves from it. She took off Odolf's shirt, buttoned all the buttons down the front, and tied the shirt cuffs around the narrow end of the limb. Then she held the limb high over her head and waved it back and forth like a flag.

Although the shirt was too grubby to be called white anymore, the color was still light enough to contrast with the dark jungle behind her. As she waved the flag from side to side, air billowed inside the shirt, making it puff out. She waved the flag in a figure eight design, causing the shirt to swoop and climb.

She was certain the captain or the first mate would look through a telescope toward shore. They would want to see the land they were passing, just as Captain Bacon and the crew of the *Black Lightning* had. A more reputable ship might even have more than one telescope.

Emma thought the movement of the flag would catch the eye of anyone who looked her direction. Once they saw her flag, they would know that she was sending a distress signal.

The rain stopped, the waves became smaller, and the black clouds moved on.

Emma's hopes soared even higher and faster than her flag. No matter where the ship was headed, she believed it would respond to her plea for help and pick her up. It could anchor offshore and send a small rowboat to get her.

When it's close enough, Emma thought, I'll swim out to it if I have to, and climb up the side as if it were a tree.

Emma thought how luxurious it would be to have a dry bed to sleep on. And food! After two weeks of figs and termites, even cold beans and black coffee would taste like a feast.

She wondered about the ship's destination. She knew she would have to go wherever the ship was headed, but once there, she could board a different vessel back to Liverpool. The captain would surely help her make arrangements to get home.

The ship crept along the rim of the horizon going from right to left until it was straight out from Emma. Although it moved at a steady pace, it came no closer to shore. Emma knew it was too far away for her to swim to it.

The sun broke out of the clouds, directly overhead. Wisps of steam rose from the ground. Behind her in the jungle, birds chattered and cawed.

Emma's arms ached from swinging the flag back and forth. Her temples throbbed with a worsening headache, and her energy lagged. I should have eaten, she thought.

Still, she did not want to leave long enough to get food. What if she left and that was the one minute when someone on board the ship aimed the telescope toward her?

Why doesn't it sail this way? Emma wondered. By now the telescope should have scanned the shoreline a dozen times. Don't they see me?

Or do they see me and have chosen not to rescue me?

No! Emma refused to think that. They would rescue her. They had to.

"Help me!" she shouted, although she knew her words would not be heard on board. "You can't just pass by and leave me here! Come and get me!"

The ship moved steadily to Emma's left, getting farther away now instead of closer. She continued to wave the flag, not knowing what else to do, as tears of despair trickled down her cheeks. The sun beat down on Emma's shoulders.

As the ship grew smaller, Emma's headache got larger. She was too hot standing in the sun. She began to feel sick to her stomach, and dizzy.

When the ship was once again only a tiny spot on the horizon, now far to her left, she untied the shirt, flung the branch to the ground in frustration, and started back into the jungle.

Her head spun when she walked, and her knees felt weak. The thought of food, even a plump ripe fig, made her gag.

Although bright sunshine filtered through the trees, Emma felt suddenly chilled. In all of her days and nights in the jungle, wet or dry, she had never been cold. Now her teeth chattered and her body shook with shivers.

Something is wrong with me, Emma realized. It isn't hunger that's making my head hurt. I'm getting sick.

Holding on to the trees for support, she headed toward her shelter. If she was ill, she needed to lie down where she had water and could sleep protected from the rain.

Before she reached the shelter, her legs buckled.

Emma lay on the ground, trembling. Have I eaten a poisonous plant? she wondered. Did one of the mosquitoes pass on a disease when it bit me? Did I drink dirty water?

She tried to stand up, but a wave of nausea washed over her and she lay down again.

The sweat that dripped from her brow was different from the ordinary sweat caused by the warm days with high humidity. This sweat felt cold and clammy.

Emma lay still until the nausea passed, then crawled on her hands and knees toward her shelter.

Her head throbbed, and she was glad she had not eaten breakfast because she knew anything in her stomach now would come back up.

She had never felt so tired, not even during those first days on board the *Black Lightning* when she did such hard physical work.

Her muscles ached so that it took every bit of willpower she had to creep forward.

She saw her shelter a few yards ahead and struggled toward it.

The dizziness grew worse. Emma stopped to rest, lowering her head toward the ground.

Before her forehead touched the earth, she passed out.

CHAPTER
14

——⟨∞⟩——

WHEN EMMA WOKE up, her breath came in rapid gasps. Even though she lay in the shade, she felt as if she were burning up. She did not know how long she had been unconscious.

She remembered when Mama first got sick, Mama's fever had shot up to one hundred and three degrees. Dr. Crissy had come; he had told Mattie and Papa to soak cloths in cold water and put them on Mama's forehead.

The cloths warmed quickly and had to be replaced with fresh ones. Emma was kept busy filling pans with cold water and carrying them to Mama's room.

Papa had spooned spirit of saffron into Mama's mouth, urging her to swallow. When Mama shook with cold despite her fever, Mattie had covered her with a quilt.

Do I have what Mama had? Emma wondered. First I was cold and now I'm hot. She did not remember Mama's breath coming fast. Emma felt as if she had just run miles and miles uphill and couldn't get enough air. Her heart fluttered like a candle flame in a breeze.

I can't have consumption, Emma told herself. I'm alone in a jungle, with no one to take care of me.

She started to sit up, moaned, and put her head back on the ground. She drifted into a dreamless sleep. Each time she opened her eyes, she felt hotter and more weary. She was too weak even to shift position.

Once she jerked awake, aware of a crawling sensation on her left arm. She raised her head and saw a green lizard creeping up her arm toward her shoulder.

She had seen lizards in the jungle several times and had always watched them with interest. But it was one thing to observe a lizard as it sunned itself on a rock or ambled across a fallen log. It was entirely different to feel the lizard's feet, and its tail dragging behind, as it marched up her arm.

Emma shook her arm to get the lizard off. Instead of falling onto the ground, the lizard landed on Emma's chest.

She batted at it, hitting its tail and knocking

the lizard down toward her legs. The lizard scuttled across her knee and onto the ground.

Emma flopped her head back down, wondering what else might crawl on her. She had seen only one snake in the jungle, and it had been small, but she had often seen rats scurrying in the undergrowth, and she didn't know what creatures moved about after dark. Twice she had watched bats, just after sunset, swooping from tree to tree.

She didn't think the chimpanzees would harm her, and she had not seen the buffalo since that first day, but there could be other animals—fierce, people-eating animals—who would sense her helplessness and pounce.

Emma's eyes closed. She was too sick even to worry.

Night came, followed by another day. Emma's mouth was as dry as it had been when she rode the waves on her hatch cover, far from shore. Feeling as if her body were on fire, she longed for a drink of water.

She knew she was only a short distance from her water basket, but she was unable to drag herself to it.

She did not stay awake long. Most of the time she tossed restlessly in her sleep.

It rained twice, but few drops fell through the canopy of trees under which Emma lay, and the showers passed quickly.

Late on the second afternoon of her fever,

Emma dozed and woke and dozed some more, thinking she would surely die of thirst soon. She moaned, unable to get comfortable.

As she sank toward unconsciousness again, a dribble of water trickled across her mouth. Rain, Emma thought, as she licked her lips. She tried to rouse herself.

Soon more water drizzled on her lips. She opened her mouth gratefully.

It isn't raining, Emma realized as the liquid ran down her throat. No rain drops were splashing on her arms or her legs or anywhere else except her mouth.

She opened her eyes. The mother chimp sat beside her. The baby chimp crouched next to his mother, staring curiously at Emma.

The mother held her fist directly over Emma's face and squeezed. Water dripped down. Emma opened her mouth again, and the mother chimp aimed the water there.

When no more water came, the chimp opened her fist, and Emma saw that she held a handful of green leaves that had been mashed into a ball. As Emma watched, the chimp moved to a large log that lay parallel to Emma, and shoved the wad of leaves into a hole. When she removed it, water dripped through her fingers.

Quickly the chimp put the soggy leaves over Emma's face and squeezed them again, sending another stream into Emma's open mouth.

She's made a sponge, Emma thought in astonishment. She's soaking up water that collected in that log, and then she's emptying it for me to drink.

The second time the chimp opened her fist, Emma saw teeth marks in the leaves. She realized the chimp must have chewed the leaves in order to mash them up.

Ordinarily the idea of drinking water from a mess of leaves that a chimpanzee had chewed and spit out would have disgusted Emma. Not now. She welcomed every drop of water that dripped into her mouth. Emma believed that without it, she would have died.

The chimp repeated the process until no more water soaked into her wad. Then she ambled around, her baby following like a shadow, until she found another source.

The chimp stayed with Emma until it began to grow dark, bringing water the entire time. Gradually Emma's thirst was quenched. At dusk the mother dropped the wad of leaves, picked up her baby, and started to walk away.

"Thank you," Emma whispered.

The chimp looked back, apparently surprised that Emma could make a sound.

"Thank you," Emma repeated.

The chimp hurried off into the trees.

Some time in the night Emma knew her temperature had dropped. Oddly, she began to sweat, although she had not when her body felt on fire. Now, with the fever gone, her clothes were drenched and her hair stuck to the sides of her face. She removed Odolf's shirt.

By morning she felt better, and as soon as it was light she crawled into her shelter. She picked up her water basket and saw that the water had turned green at the edges. Hating to waste it but afraid to drink it, Emma poured it on the ground.

She discarded the leaves that lined the basket, too. She would need to line the basket with fresh ones before she used it again but that would have to wait. The effort of returning to her shelter had exhausted her; Emma went back to sleep.

A commotion outside the shelter woke her. Emma saw the mother chimp and two other chimps tossing something in the air while the baby jumped with excitement. Emma looked closer. The chimps were playing with Odolf's shirt.

Emma remembered taking it off in the night, when she was so hot. She had left it outside the shelter.

The chimps seemed delighted with their treasure. They passed it around; even the baby got a turn to examine it. One chimp chewed on a sleeve for a while, another draped the shirt over her head like a scarf. Their bright eyes, the ways they used their hands, and the curious expressions on their faces all resembled a group of children playing with a new toy.

Emma needed the shirt for nighttime protection from the mosquitoes, but she did not dare to try to take it away from the chimps. She hoped they would eventually tire of it and leave it where they had found it.

After a few minutes the chimps noticed Emma watching them. The other two adults backed away, but the mother chimp stayed where she was. She's no longer afraid of me, Emma thought. Before long the two other chimps edged close to the mother chimp and hugged her, as if seeking reassurance. Then they returned to their game, although they continued to watch Emma.

The chimps were still there when hunger drove Emma from her shelter. She had eaten nothing during her sickness, and now she desperately needed food. Trying not to alarm the chimps, she eased out of her shelter and backed slowly away from them. When she moved they hurried into the woods, taking Odolf's shirt with them.

Emma drank the rainwater that had collected in shallow pools in the fallen trees. She tore leaves from branches and chewed them. Her stomach contracted in painful cramps. She wondered if any of the plant roots were edible. She pulled up a small sapling, brushed away the dirt that clung to its roots, and bit off a piece of root. It was pithy and bitter; Emma chewed a long time before she swallowed.

She knew she needed more than leaves and roots. A slight movement on the ground caught her eye. Are lizards poisonous? she wondered. She dropped to her knees, lunging toward the movement, but her hands came up empty.

A new idea struck her: perhaps there were fish close to shore. She carried her water basket to the ocean's edge, wondering if any ships had passed while she had been sick. She lay on her stomach and thrust the basket down until the water reached her armpit. Then she pulled the basket sideways and up, hoping to catch a fish. She repeated the motion many times but re-trieved only a small bit of seaweed, which she ate.

Wearily, she scanned the horizon as she had done so many times before. She yearned to hear another human voice. Even Cook's harsh orders or Odolf's taunts would be better than this un-ending loneliness.

I can't go on much longer, Emma thought. I'll starve to death here in the jungle or die of a sick-ness, and no one will ever find me. Mama and Papa will never know what happened to me.

When she was too tired to fish any longer, she returned to her shelter, chewing leaves as she went. Weakened from the fever, her legs felt wobbly. Rain splattered down, but it was a gen-tle, warm shower, and Emma no longer cared if she got wet. What difference did it make?

As she dropped to her knees to crawl into her shelter, she saw a bit of yellow color on the ground where the chimps had been. Emma picked it up and recognized the stem end of a banana. In the excitement over the shirt, one of the chimps must have dropped it.

Saliva sprang to Emma's mouth. If there was one banana, there were more. Emma needed only to find the banana trees.

The banana stem brought back Emma's determination. She rested until her legs quit trembling, and then set off. This time she did not stay in the area she knew so well; she had already found any food in this part of the jungle.

For the first time since she had startled the buffalo, she went into the sword-sharp grass of the meadow. Beyond it she saw more palm trees and different kinds of ferns. As she moved through the tall grass, her ears strained for any sounds and her eyes scanned the ground ahead of her.

On the far side of the meadow she looked up often, searching the treetops for a glimpse of yellow. Emma had no idea what a banana tree looked like, so she scrutinized the branches of every tree she passed. She recognized a fig tree, but it bore no fruit.

Then, just ahead, a clump of small green bananas hung high in a tree. Emma licked her lips in anticipation. She climbed the tree and yanked the whole clump free. She pulled the peel from a banana and bit into the hard fruit.

Real food, Emma thought, not caring that the banana wasn't ripe. She made herself chew thoroughly before she swallowed.

She finished the first banana, then ate the peel, too. Any food was too precious to waste. She devoured two bananas while she balanced in the tree, and carried the rest of them to the ground.

She sat at the base of the tree, clutching her prize. To her left she saw another banana tree with a clump of green bananas near the top of its trunk.

I was too cautious, Emma thought, staying near my shelter all the time because I feared the buffalo and other large animals. I nearly starved to death because I was too timid to venture beyond the meadow.

There *is* food in the jungle, and I will hunt until I find it.

CHAPTER

15

———◦◦◦———

Hunger was her constant companion. She searched for food in new parts of the jungle, going farther from her shelter each day. She found more bananas, sprays of sweet red berries on a low-growing bush, and tart purple fruit on a tree, but it was never enough.

Despite her meager diet, her muscles grew strong again from hiking and tree climbing.

She saw the chimps often and enjoyed watching them. Although they no longer ran off when they spotted her, they didn't approach her, either.

Their similarities to people always made her smile. The small ones frequently ran to their mothers and touched them, as if for comfort or encouragement. Once she was amazed to see a large male chimp jump up, rush toward a new-comer to the group, and kiss him on the lips, as if greeting him after a long absence.

She felt less lonely when she was near the chimps and sometimes watched their grooming sessions. They often sat for an hour or more, carefully searching through each other's fur for flakes of dry skin or twigs or ticks. Although she saw the chimps nearly every day, she never saw Odolf's shirt again.

Each morning and evening she went to the shore to look for a passing ship. If her search for food didn't take her too far inland, she went to the shore at midday, also. She worried that a ship might pass while she searched for food. It could be close enough to rescue her and not know she was there.

While she watched for ships, she fished with her basket. She never caught a fish, but it gave her something to do while she scanned the hori-zon, and she did sometimes bring up seaweed in her basket.

One day she broke inch-thick branches into pieces and laid them on the ground to form the letter *H*. It was two feet tall. She got more branches and made *E*, *L*, and *P*.

Next she searched for long, flexible vines which she used as rope to bind the pieces of each letter together. It took twelve tries before the *E* held its shape but Emma persisted. If this idea worked, a passing ship would know someone was here even if Emma was inland at the time.

Using more small vines, she hung her letters from a tree branch that extended along the water's edge. The letters dangled unevenly, but they formed the word *HELP*.

When the wind blew, the letters flapped up and down until it was impossible to tell what the word said. But on still days the word *HELP* was clear. Anyone looking through a telescope would know the letters were not there by accident.

Three times a storm blew one of the letters away in the night, and Emma had to replace it the next morning.

She dreamed of food: crisp apples and warm bread and roasted chestnuts. She dreamed of Mama and Papa, and once of Mattie, and of her home in England. One night she dreamed that she and Mama were singing together when Mama suddenly stopped and pleaded, "Come home, my darling girl. Come home."

Emma woke with tears streaming down her cheeks. Oh, Mama, she whispered, I wish I could.

The next morning Emma again spotted a ship on the horizon. Quickly she checked to be sure her four letters hung in place. She stepped out of Odolf's tattered trousers, and tied them to a branch to make another flag. She stood in her undergarments beside the word *HELP*, waving the flag.

This ship was sailing the opposite direction from the first ship she had seen. It's heading north, Emma realized, the way I need to go. She waved the flag vigorously.

About half an hour after Emma first saw it, the ship slowly turned and headed toward shore. Emma jumped up and down, still waving her flag, as the ship drew nearer.

It's coming! she thought. They see me and they're coming to rescue me!

Hope and relief and joy mixed together inside Emma until every nerve tingled with happiness and excitement.

The ship stopped about a hundred yards off-shore. The crew eased a small rowboat over the side. Two men, looking as if they were tiny toy figures in the distance, climbed down a rope ladder and sat in the rowboat.

The small boat moved closer, until Emma clearly saw the men. One manned the oars while the other looked at her through a telescope. Emma untied the trousers and put them back on. She waved her hands, criss-crossing them over her head.

When the rowboat was about two hundred feet away, the man with the telescope shouted, "Can you hear me?"

"Yes!" Emma called.

"Are you alone?"

"Yes!"

A wave caught the rowboat and lifted it.

Emma feared the small boat might capsize, but the two men managed to hang on and keep it upright as it plunged down again.

Instead of waiting any longer for the men to reach her, Emma jumped into the water. Kicking her feet furiously and raising her arms forward and over her head, she swam toward the rowboat.

The waves pushed her back toward shore but Emma, determined, continued to swim. The sailors stroked their oars faster, propelling the small boat toward Emma. She kept her eyes closed against the sea water. After a few minutes she stopped swimming and, treading water, looked to see where she was.

The rowboat moved toward her, only a few yards away.

"Grab the oar!"

The rowboat bobbed beside her as one of the sailors extended the oar toward her. Emma grasped it and felt herself drawn through the water. Her hands closed on the side of the wooden boat. One man stayed on the opposite side for balance while the other lifted her over the edge.

"Thank you," she said, gasping to catch her breath. "Thank you, thank you, thank you for coming to get me."

"Who are you?"

"Emma Bolton. I live outside of Liverpool, with my parents."

"And what were you doing alone in the jungle, Miss Emma?"

As they rowed her back to their ship, which she learned was a cargo ship called the *Explorer*, Emma briefly explained. She told her tale in full to the captain, and again that evening when the captain assembled the whole crew to hear her astonishing tale.

Each time she repeated her story, Emma thanked all of them again for rescuing her.

"Might your father be John Bolton?" Captain Whitworth asked.

"Yes!" Emma exclaimed. "Do you know him?"

"We have done business," Captain Whitworth said. "He is a fine gentleman."

The *Explorer* was bound for Dublin, but Captain Whitworth told Emma he would stop at Liverpool first and let her disembark there.

Tears of joy dampened Emma's cheeks. Home! At long last she was headed home.

She dined on boiled potatoes, applesauce, and a bit of hard cheese. No meal ever tasted better.

"Do you have a ship's boy?" Emma asked Captain Whitworth.

"No."

"Then I shall earn my passage," Emma declared.

"I cannot allow you to work, Miss Emma," Captain Whitworth said. "You are a young lady."

"I want to repay your kindness."

"Your father is a respected man of business. What would he say?"

"My father is not here," Emma replied.

The smallest sailor on board brought a set of his clothes to Emma's room. "They aren't lady's things," he said apologetically, "but they're clean, and they'll serve better than what you have."

When the sailor left, Emma removed the remains of Odolf's tattered trousers. They were no longer fit even for scrub rags, so she dropped them over the railing. As they floated toward shore, she remembered how excited the chimps had been over Odolf's shirt. She hoped these trousers might drift ashore where the chimps would find them.

Although the crew treated her with great courtesy, and Captain Whitworth protested if he saw her working, Emma found jobs to do. She noticed a torn sail and mended it. She entered the galley early each morning and offered to carry coffee to the men on watch. She rolled out biscuit dough, stirred the stew, and stayed to wash dishes after every meal.

Two days after her rescue, a sudden squall sent waves crashing over the *Explorer*'s rails. Without being told what to do, Emma rushed to close the porthole shutters and lash down supplies.

By the time the ship approached Liverpool, Emma was a respected member of the crew.

When they docked, Captain Whitworth insisted on sending one of his men to purchase a dress for Emma to wear home. "It will be enough of a shock for your father to see you," he said, "without having you appear in sailor's garb."

Emma waited impatiently until the sailor returned. He proudly gave her a pink ruffled gown with lace at the throat and sleeves. Emma put it on and then went on deck to show the crew. When they saw her, they burst into cheers.

Emma said good-bye to each in turn, thanking them again for saving her.

"Are you sure you don't want one of my men to accompany you, Miss Emma?" Captain Whitworth asked.

"It isn't necessary. It's a short distance and I know my way." She smiled at him. "I will always remember your kindness to me."

"It was my pleasure," Captain Whitworth said.

At midday the Liverpool docks bustled with activity. The street merchants did a brisk business; one ship loaded passengers while a stream of people disembarked from another. How different it all seemed now than it had when Emma sneaked on board the *Black Lightning* only four months earlier.

Four months. As she descended the walkway to the dock, she wondered how such a short time could change her life so drastically.

When she left she was a headstrong, impetuous child. Yes, Emma admitted, her governess had been right about that.

And now? Who am I now? Emma wondered.

No longer little Emma, Mama's darling girl. But not yet Emma the grown woman, either.

When her feet stepped onto firm ground, she waved to the crew of the *Explorer.*

Despite her assurances to Captain Whitworth she was not certain how to find Aunt Martha's house. It had been so dark the night she left that she had not noticed any landmarks, and the last half of the way to the docks she had followed the street boy rather than paying close attention.

She knew the general direction, and she had plenty of daylight. If I could survive a journey on the *Black Lightning,* she told herself, and live alone in the wilds of Africa, I should be able to find my aunt's house in the city of Liverpool.

Emma was eager for news of Mama, but she also dreaded what that news might be. At least she would finally know. Even if the news was bad, it was better than not knowing.

CHAPTER

16

—⟨o/o/o⟩—

THE SLUMS SEEMED less frightening in daylight. Or perhaps it was that she had lived in such deplorable conditions herself that the ramshackle buildings and the filth no longer shocked her.

Many children played in the streets. Emma looked for the boy who had led her to the docks, but did not see him.

Just when she thought she might be going the wrong way, she saw the alehouse where she had tricked the drunken men.

Sure of her direction now, Emma walked faster. Soon she passed tidy homes with well-kept gardens. Then, just ahead, she recognized a home belonging to one of Aunt Martha's friends, and she knew Aunt Martha's house was two blocks over.

Emma ran the rest of the way, took the steps two at a time, and knocked on Aunt Martha's door. Seconds later Aunt Martha opened it.

"Emma!" she gasped, and drew Emma inside.

"Are you all right, Emma?" Aunt Martha said. "Where have you been? Why didn't you contact us?" She hugged Emma briefly, then stepped back and scrutinized her niece. "You are different," she said. "Your hair has been cut, and you are leaner. What has happened to you?"

"How is Mama?" Emma asked.

"She is better," Aunt Martha said.

Relief poured through Emma, washing away the fear that had clung to the back of her mind for four long months. Mama was better! "Is she home? Have they returned?"

"No. They expect to be in France several more months." Aunt Martha spoke slowly, as if weighing each word before it left her lips. She seemed glad to see Emma, but at the same time she appeared nervous. The color had drained from her face, and instead of looking directly at Emma, she gazed over the top of Emma's head.

"I must write to them immediately," Emma said, "to let them know I am safe."

"That—that won't be necessary," Aunt Martha said.

Again, Emma puzzled at her aunt's uneasiness. "I can't let them continue to worry about me," Emma said.

"They are not worried."

"But—"

"Your papa sent word last week that they would like you to join them."

It took a moment for the full meaning of Papa's message to become clear. Emma looked at her aunt in disbelief.

"Mama and Papa do not know I've been away?" Emma asked. "You did not tell them?"

Aunt Martha looked down. "I felt it best not to alarm your mother." Aunt Martha's fingers fidgeted with the hem of her apron.

Incredulous, Emma stared at her aunt. She understood that worry might not be good for Mama, but surely the choice of whether or not to tell Mama should have been Papa's decision, not Aunt Martha's.

It was unthinkable that Papa was never told that Emma had disappeared. All this time, while Emma battled for her life, Papa and Mama had thought she was here with Aunt Martha.

Emma remembered Odolf's statement that the only reason his mother took Emma in was because Papa paid her to do so. Was it possible, Emma wondered, that Aunt Martha didn't tell Papa I was missing so that he would continue to send money each month for my care? Had Aunt Martha spent the money, even though I was not here?

Emma could think of no other explanation. Yet she knew that if Aunt Martha needed money, Papa would gladly have given it. He had done so in the past. Could Aunt Martha be telling the truth, that she had withheld such important information in an effort to protect Mama? There was only one way to find out.

"Could I please have the funds that Papa sent you for my care?" Emma said. "Since they were not needed, I'll return them to Papa to pay for my passage to France."

The smile disappeared from Aunt Martha's face. "I'm afraid that isn't possible," she said.

Emma waited for an explanation.

"Now that you are safely back," Aunt Martha continued, "we must pretend you've been with me all along." Her eyes pleaded with Emma to agree. "To avoid upsetting your mother," she added.

Emma knew that when Mama was well, she would tell her parents the whole truth of what had happened. She could not imagine keeping her adventure a secret from Mama.

But the prospect of joining her family in France without having to face Papa's anger at her for running away was tempting. Papa and Mama would be happier believing Emma had been safe with Aunt Martha these four months. They could learn later of the terrible dangers she had faced.

Emma chose her words carefully. "I agree," she said, "that it would be best not to upset Mama."

"We did look for you," Aunt Martha said. "Odolf and I tried to find you. And each day I hoped you would return."

Even so, Emma felt betrayed. How long had they looked? And where? Aunt Martha had not alerted Captain Forbes of the *Wayfarer* to look for her on board; if she had, Papa would have known about Emma's absence.

"This can remain our little secret," Aunt Martha said. She smoothed the front of her dress over and over. "Even when your mother has recovered, it would distress her to learn you were not here for so many weeks."

Emma refused to lie, just to make Aunt Martha feel less guilty. She knew she would one day tell her parents everything that had happened.

Her relief at being back in Liverpool and her joy at knowing Mama was improving had become an intense desire to leave Aunt Martha's house as soon as possible.

"How soon can we book passage for me to sail to France?" Emma asked. "Did Papa send money for my fare?" She almost added, "Or have you spent that, too?" but restrained herself.

"Your father made the arrangements from Bordeaux. You are to sail day after tomorrow on the *Wayfarer*, with the same captain who took your parents."

What did Aunt Martha plan to do if I had not returned in time? Emma wondered. Would she have finally told Papa the truth, when it was far too late for him to find me? Or would she have lied and told him that I preferred to stay in Liverpool? Aunt Martha might have continued to accept and spend the funds Papa sent each month. When he and Mama finally came home, she could then pretend that I had only recently disappeared.

"Your hair is short," Aunt Martha said.

Emma offered no explanation for her haircut. She intended to say as little as possible about her journey, or anything else. She wanted only to leave as soon as she could and be reunited with her parents.

"Is my trunk still here?" she asked, worried that it might be gone and its contents sold.

"It's where you left it."

"Good. Then I am prepared to sail day after to-morrow."

Aunt Martha never again asked where Emma had been or what had happened to her. It was as if by pretending Emma had never been gone, she would make it true.

Odolf, however, could not contain his curiosity. As soon as he and Emma were alone, he said, "You didn't go to stay with a friend, did you? You have callouses on your hands and your skin is brown from the sun."

What would Odolf say, she wondered, if I told him I had stowed away on a slave ship, survived a shipwreck, lay unconscious in the jungles of Africa, and been nursed back to health by a mother chimpanzee?

Emma hugged her memories close. Now that

she was safely back in Liverpool, her secret journey seemed more thrilling than frightening.

"Well?" Odolf said. "Where were you?"

"I went to Africa," Emma said. "I lived in the jungle and ate termites." Her eyes twinkled at the look of disbelief on Odolf's face.

"You once called me a liar," Odolf said, "but now you're the one who's lying."

"Do you consider it honest," Emma said, "to take the money sent for my care and not tell my parents I had left? How long would that lie have continued if I had not returned?"

"You take that back!" Odolf said. He grabbed for Emma's arm, to twist it behind her, but Emma caught his hand and pushed it away.

Odolf blinked in surprise; his face flushed with anger. He lunged at Emma. She put both hands on his shoulders and shoved him so hard that he stumbled backward, hitting his head against the wall.

"Don't ever touch me again," she said.

He stood facing her, rubbing his head with one hand. He made no further attempt to hurt her. "Your hair is ugly," he said.

"Yes, it is," Emma agreed cheerfully. "But it will grow."

"You will hate sailing to France," he said. "The rooms on ships are small and the vessels move up and down with the waves. You'll be seasick for weeks."

Emma burst out laughing.

Odolf stomped away. Emma knew he would never tease her again.

Maury's words came again to Emma's mind: *Some good comes of every difficulty.*

She opened her trunk and removed a dress. When she had packed it four months earlier, she was still a child. She put it on and gazed at her reflection in the mirror. The dress hung more loosely than it used to.

Her slender frame, her uneven haircut, and her tanned skin were small changes. The big difference in Emma was on the inside.

She wondered if Mama would notice that her darling girl was now strong and bold and capable.

She wondered what Papa would say when he eventually learned that Aunt Martha had withheld the truth from him.

And she wondered if Captain Forbes had need of a ship's boy for the journey to France.

Author's Notes
About Research

—⟨∂∕∂⟩—

Although *The Secret Journey* is fiction, I tried to be accurate with all the information I included. The following books were particularly useful.

Clipper Ships and Captains
by Jane Lyon
HarperCollins

The Rain Forests of West Africa
by Claude Martin
Birkhauser

My Friends, the Wild Chimpanzees
by Jane Goodall
National Geographic Society

Goblin, a Wild Chimpanzee
by Teleki and Steffy
Dutton

*A Writer's Guide to Everyday Life in
Regency and Victorian England from
1811–1901*
by Kristine Hughes
F & W Publications, Inc.

Jane Goodall is known worldwide as an authority on chimpanzees. I read several of her books in order to grasp the behavior of these magnificent creatures, and I gratefully acknowledge her life's work. She has written *My Life with the Chimpanzees* for young readers, published by Minstrel Books, an imprint of Pocket Books.

Mike Wallace of the National Oceanic and Atmospheric Administration (NOAA) helped me understand how the ocean behaves in the area I wrote about. He also told me details about water temperatures and shorelines. Before I talked to Mike, I had spent many hours trying, without success, to find out what the ocean temperature would have been at the time and place of Emma's shipwreck. I thank him for his help.

Much of a writer's research never shows, but it is important nevertheless. A book called *Coins of the World, 1750–1850,* by W. D. Craig, helped me decide what coin the seaman would offer to the boys who caught his chickens.

Ted Wyder of the University of Washington Department of Astronomy told me which constellations Emma would see at that time and place.

I also read medical books so that I could correctly describe the symptoms of malaria, even though my book never states what was wrong with Emma when she fell sick.

Such research is an exciting part of the writing process for me; I learned a great deal as I wrote *The Secret Journey.*

About the Author

PEG KEHRET's books for young readers are regularly recommended by the American Library Association, the International Reading Association, and the Children's Book Council. She has won "children's choice" awards in fourteen states and has also won the Golden Kite Award from the Society of Children's Book Writers & Illustrators and the PEN Center West Award for Children's Literature. A longtime volunteer at the Humane Society, she often uses animals in her stories.

Peg and her husband, Carl, live in a log house on ten acres of forest near Mount Rainier National Park. Their property is a sanctuary for blacktail deer, elk, rabbits, and many kinds of birds. They have two grown children, four grandchildren, a dog, and two cats. When she is not writing, Peg likes to read, watch baseball, and pump her old player piano.